Beneath the Shame

Broken Boys, Volume 3

Zane Menzy

Published by Zane Menzy, 2023.

This is a work of fiction. Similarities to real people, places, or events are entirely coincidental.

BENEATH THE SHAME

First edition. October 23, 2023.

Copyright © 2023 Zane Menzy.

ISBN: 979-8223901822

Written by Zane Menzy.

Chapter 1

AFTER LAST NIGHT'S official signing and handing over of the contract, I had awoken this morning feeling a bit spaced out. Jockey hadn't stayed long after dumping his load inside me, and he hadn't bothered getting me off in return. As long as the muscles of my ass sucked the sperm out of his cock, that was all that mattered apparently. I existed for his pleasure now, not mine.

After wiping his dick clean on my blanket, he'd pulled his pants up, gave my ass a slap, and told me he would text me when he was ready to do my inspection—a procedure he'd described as "A testing of your honesty."

He would discover I had been honest. Well...mostly honest. It wasn't that I had lied while filling out the questions contained within the contract but there were a couple that had seen me withhold the full details. The main one being where I'd been asked to disclose my full sexual history. After writing down Jockey himself as a sex partner, I'd listed how there had been one time when I'd sucked a bloke off at a park. I did not name the park and I certainly did not name the man. And in my defence, the contract had not asked me to give names.

The last thing I wanted was to have Jockey find out I'd received sexual relief at Hickford Park, Moa Hill's notorious cruising spot.

While I wasn't sure if my blowjob was enough to have me labelled a *Hickford Homo* I still didn't want people knowing about it. I also didn't want Jockey knowing that I had sucked off Brian's father. Aside from the endless mocking that would earn me I didn't want to risk Jockey passing the story on and it somehow getting back to Brian or Mrs Quale. Rowan Quayle may have been a dirty fiend with an unhealthy interest in his son—and his son's smelly sneakers—but I had no interest in making that public knowledge.

Lying in bed, I dipped a hand between my legs and gently probed my asshole. It didn't hurt as much as the first time Jockey had fucked me but I was certainly tender down there. And wet. The other part of my body that was sore was my scalp from where Jockey had pulled on my hair as he railed my ass. I'd always taken great pride in my long hair, liked to think it added a bit of grungy rebel to my image, but now that piece of pride had been reduced to a convenient set of fuck handles.

"Jockey owns me," I whispered to myself. It was trippy to say out loud and left me lightheaded.

It wasn't regret I was experiencing, or at least I don't think that's what it was, it was more a case of foggy disbelief. My signature was now on a piece of paper that gave Jockey Savage ownership of my body for the next twelve months. One whole year of being at the sexual mercy of a scruffy stoner most of the town considered a social pariah. The thought should have terrified me more than it actually did, but I knew I had done what felt necessary—obtaining some stability.

While the contract did not come into effect for another seven days, Jockey had written down a list of websites he expected me to look up before the commencement date so that I would have a better idea about my new role as a faggot. I'd nodded politely and promised him I would, even though the thought of studying for my role seemed silly. How hard could it be? He would call me homophobic slurs and got to fuck me whenever he pleased. It wasn't rocket science.

As I rolled out of bed, I thought about how he'd told me to make the most of the next seven days. It hadn't been said in a threatening manner but it had carried an ominous tone. However, it was something else Jockey said that had bothered me more, an innocent off the cuff remark that had cut my ego, "It's a shame you never got a chance to be a man. Just went straight from boy to bitch."

While being called a bitch didn't thrill me it wasn't the part that had pissed me off. It was how Jockey had still considered me a boy before fucking me. Seriously? Just a boy? He'd been sucking my dick for the past two years, tasting my spunk more than once. Surely that constituted me being a man. Granted, I was lean in build, a body still maturing, but I was hairy where I was supposed to be and my balls had dropped years ago.

I pulled on yesterday's underwear, grabbed my phone, and made my way to the kitchen for a cup of coffee to help wake me up. I got a shock to see Gavin sat at the table while he read the newspaper. He had on blue overalls and a pair of grey woolly socks; his usual attire when he intended to work on Betsy after breakfast. It didn't matter if it was tinkering with the motor or fixing a cabinet inside the old girl's interior, Gavin always wore these overalls like he was living some sort of mechanic fantasy.

The next thing that surprised me was the overpowering stench of incense. Feigning more annoyance than I actually felt, I blurted, "Why does it smell like a gypsy's armpit in here?"

"Because Fiona's coming over later." Gavin lowered the newspaper. "She loves the smell of lavender."

"I hope so because it's at toxic levels in here." I then glanced around the messy state of the kitchen and took a not-so subtle jab, "She might prefer a clean cup to drink out of rather than the smell of lavender."

"It's not that bad." He looked over at the cluttered kitchen bench. "Is it?"

It *was* that bad but I dismissed his question with a shrug, worried that he might ask me to wash up the growing pile of dishes.

While I filled up the kettle, Gavin sat there smirking at me. I wondered what he found so amusing until I glanced down at my naked chest and saw that it was marked like a purple-spotted dalmatian. *Jockey Savage strikes again.*

My tummy dropped to my toes, hoping Gavin wouldn't verbalise is smirk.

That wishful thought detonated within two seconds when he let out a long, slow wolf whistle. "Did someone's sexy vampire stay over last night?"

"They may have paid a short visit."

"A short visit." He snorted. "Ain't nothing *short visit* about those marks ya filthy man whore."

I felt my cheeks begin to redden.

He rolled his eyes, dismissing my embarrassment. "So when do I get to meet the little minx?"

"Um...."

"You should invite her round for dinner one night. I could invite Fiona over and do a double date sort of thing."

I was sort of flattered that Gavin viewed me adult enough to include in a double date. Pity it could never happen. "I'll ask her next time I see her."

"Make sure you do. I'm keen to see how fucking sharp those teeth are in person." Gavin stared again at my torso, his gaze dipping as low as my crotch. "Just how bloody low do those marks go?"

"About as low as your standards," I quipped.

That made him laugh but his expression soon turned serious. "I hope you used a condom like we talked about. You don't want to end up a daddy before your time."

"No one got pregnant last night."

"That doesn't answer my question. Did you use a condom?"

I hesitated, not wanting to lie.

Gavin sighed and his shoulders sagged, like everything was just too fucking heavy. "Bloody hell, Mike. You gotta be smarter than that. It don't matter if she's on the pill you still gotta wrap it up, buddy."

Rather than argue over the dangers of an unwanted pregnancy that was never going to happen, I just nodded and took the lecture, which went on and on and fucking on. The dude meant well but it did get on my tits, which is why when I eventually joined him at the table with my cup of coffee, I decided it was my turn to take the piss out of his sex life. "How is it going adjusting to life as a caged animal?"

"Huh?"

"The cock cage," I started, raising my eyebrows. "Have you still got it on?"

"I sure do."

"You sound pretty chill about it. I thought you'd have been a bit more rattled by now."

"It's only been twenty-four hours. Ask me in a couple more days and I might be a little more stressed about it." His hand headed south in the direction of his crotch, the look on his face gave away he was fingering the cage. "I reckon the government should make these things mandatory for teenage boys to wear to school. It would have saved me a lot of embarrassment from ill-timed boners growing up."

"Sounds like an election winner."

"I think you mean an *erection* winner."

I snorted into my coffee.

"There has been one good thing about having my dick locked up though," Gavin said.

"What's that?"

"Just how good Fiona's been treating me. For example, what she did to me this morning before I left her place. Talk about putting a smile on a man's face."

"I don't want to know—"

"Let's just say I don't need a bath today because she already gave me one." He stared at me waiting for a response he didn't get. "With her tongue. Can you believe it? Head to toe. I was licked places I never thought a tongue would go but my girl ain't afraid to get a bit freaky."

"I repeat...I don't want to know."

"Are you sure? Because I can tell you about how I returned the favour."

"Well," I said loudly, "on a less vomit-inducing topic, guess who won five-hundred dollars on a scratchie ticket?"

"You didn't?"

"I sure did. Five-hundred smackaroos."

"Good job, you. You've always been a lucky little fucker."

"Have I?"

"Don't you remember winning that skateboard when you were a kid?"

"I'd forgotten that. My Ninja Turtles skateboard."

"I also know you're lucky because whenever there's a raffle at the tavern I never win when I put in my name but I usually get something if I write down yours."

"You write my name down for competitions?"

"Yep. So far your name has won me two meat raffles and a free meal."

I laughed. "You're welcome."

"So ya lucky bugger, what are you gonna spend your winnings on?"

"I don't know yet."

"You could donate it to the Betsy fund so I can help get the old girl up and running faster."

I cast a glance in the direction of the backyard where Betsy the bus was parked motionless. "I think Betsy needs more money than what I won." I turned back to Gavin. "But you can put your half into the Betsy fund if you like?"

"My half?"

"I bought the ticket with money you gave me for dinner."

"Pfft. You won it, not me."

"Are you sure?"

"I don't need the money. I'm already the richest man in the world." He waggled his eyebrows and I knew something dirty was about to come out of his mouth. "How many men are lucky enough to have a woman lick their butthole for them?"

I grimaced, not needing to know Fiona had liked out my stepfather's hairy shitter. To be fair to Gavin, I knew first-hand how good a tongue down there felt. I wondered if Fiona had done the same to Jockey and if that's why he'd been so good at it.

My phone had a fit on the table, buzzing brightly as a text message came in.

Jockey: I want you to send me a video of you visiting your favourite place in town.

I smiled like an idiot at my phone, finding the random request oddly sweet. My man wanted to know more about me. The little text bubble appeared in the window to show that he was typing another message.

Jockey: And make sure your cock is out in the video.

Although less sweet, Jockey's demanding message spoke to me on a level I was still adjusting to. A primal level that had me discreetly reaching for my nuts under the table.

"Is that your sexy vampire?" Gavin asked. "Is she gagging for another nibble on Mikey's love muscle, is she?"

I offered a faux groan, and responded to Jockey's message with an obedient *Yes sir*. Putting my phone down, I then asked Gavin if I could borrow his car.

"Do you need it to go visit your sexy vampire?"

"Something like that."

"That's fine," he answered, then made no effort at discretion when he reached down and adjusted the cock cage in his jeans. "I won't need the car until tonight anyway."

"Thanks, Gavin."

"Funnily enough, you being out of the house for a few hours would actually be doing me a favour."

"How's that?"

"Fiona's bringing over the 'third party' for me to meet later today." He did little finger quotes.

"I'm guessing by third party you mean the dude she wants you to have a threeway with?"

"That's the one." He laughed, dry and humourless. "So it's probably best you stay out of the house for a few hours. I don't want you to hear things you shouldn't be hearing."

"Ya think?" I screwed my face up in revulsion. "Ain't no way I want to be in the house while you lot have an orgy."

"It's a threesome, Mike, not an orgy," Gavin snapped. "And no sex is happening today. We're just gonna have a chat about things...see if me and this guy gel or not."

"I'm no expert but wouldn't it be best to just drink a bottle of Smirnoff and get it over with?"

He laughed again. It wasn't as brittle this time, but neither was it joyful. "That's pretty much my thoughts on the situation but Fiona insisted it's best we get to know each other first. She said it's important we decide on some boundaries, which is probably a good idea. I don't want this bloke to get the wrong impression and think I'm down for anything too out there."

On one hand that sounded sensible but I couldn't help but feel it was just another way for sexpot Fiona to exert some control over a situation that a man like Gavin would have had no desire to be a part of had she not been bribing him with a fantasy of his own. Quite frankly though, I found Gavin's fantasy just as bizarre as hers; wanting a woman to suck him and his best mate off while they watched the first three Die-Hard films.

"So what rules are you setting in place?" I asked.

There was something irked and frosty behind his eyes, but there was also playfulness. "How come you're so interested in my threeway? Are you looking for an invite?"

I stared back with wide eyes and a gaping mouth.

"I'm joking you idiot." He sniggered. "You should see your face."

"Sorry." I took a quick sip on my coffee to try and hide my embarrassment. "I should mind my own business."

"It's okay. I'd wanna be a nosey fucker too. It's not every day a straight man tells you he's taking a ride on the Hershey highway with another bloke." His tone was laidback but I knew him too well to not sense his discomfort. "And to be honest with you, I'm still not sure what rules I wanna have in place. I guess a lot of it will depend on how today's meeting goes. If he's a good sort then maybe it will go further than I originally intended."

"Further how?"

"Well, I was thinking I might let him take the driver's seat...if you know what I mean?"

"You're gonna let the guy fuck you?"

"I'm considering it. Provided he ain't hung like a horse then it might be easier. That way I might be able to take this cunting chastity device off sooner. I've only got it on because Fiona thought it would be a way to make sure I'm horny enough to rise to the occasion. But if I'm on the receiving end then I don't need to rise to the occasion so to speak. Make sense?"

I nodded.

"And even if this guy turns out to be a fucking munter I wouldn't touch with a shitty stick then I still get something out of it."

"What's that?"

"Apparently he's good with motors. Fiona said after we've had ourselves a chat that he'll be willing to give me a hand with Betsy for the afternoon."

"Well, you know what they say. The thrupple who repair buses together fuck together."

Gavin grinned, big and warm. "Smart ass."

His grin was contagious. I caught it and let it spread. The fact we could talk at ease about something so ludicrous, so outrageous, reminded me how lucky I was to have him in my life. Nothing was off limits with this man and he didn't take himself too seriously. I think that had been good for someone like me who had a tendency to be a bit uptight and inclined to be a worry wart. My grin faded though when I realised I wouldn't have Gavin to myself for much longer. Fiona was fast-becoming his number one priority and I could already sense myself being pushed aside to make room for her and her brood.

"So what time should I aim to be back home by?" I asked.

"They should be gone by three o'clock, so any time after then."

"Cool. So you won't mind if I'm home by two o'clock so you can introduce me to your new boyfriend." When he shot me a surly look, I quickly added, "Sorry. It was a joke."

"You can come back early on the condition you don't say anything stupid. I don't want Fiona knowing I've told you about any of this. She'd be horrified if you knew."

I somehow doubted that but nodded anyway.

"And if you do plan on being a nosey fucker then I expect you to return the favour."

"Huh?" I asked, super intelligently.

"You invite your girlfriend to come for dinner next weekend. If I can introduce you to the man who might be popping my bum cherry then the least you can do is introduce me to the girl you're dating." He frowned, looking as if he'd misspoken. "You are dating, right? Or are you still just playing it by ear?"

I thought about Jockey pinning me to the bed last night, fucking me both roughly and beautifully.

"We have an arrangement," I eventually said, feeling myself grow hard beneath the table.

"An arrangement," Gavin echoed. "Sounds kinky."

You don't know the half of it.

Chapter 2

AFTER STOPPING OFF at a servo to put some gas in Gavin's car, I drove in the direction of the Moa Hill lookout—my favourite place in town. Technically it wasn't in town, or even within the city limits, but it was still considered a local attraction and probably a safe place to whip my dick out for a video.

Located in the steep ranges bordering Moa Hill, the lookout was a popular hangout in the evening for horny couples looking for some privacy and families looking for a scenic place to eat their McDonalds. It was only a ten-minute drive from where I lived, taking you from an urban landscape to a narrow winding road surrounded by native forest.

The ranges surrounding Moa Hill were a reminder of how my riverside town had once been covered in native forest. I sometimes liked to imagine how my Māori ancestors lived off the land before the arrival of my European ancestors, gathering kai from the bush, sea, rivers and lakes. The storyteller in me painted a peaceful utopia with lives revolving around sleeping, eating and fucking. Of course I knew the precolonial history of Aotearoa wasn't quite that idyllic or simple. Intertribal warfare had been common and Māori had cleared up to forty percent of the forest before a single land-hungry

European, armed with muskets and bibles and a deluded sense of their own enlightenment, had set foot on these shores.

Perhaps that's what we all had in common, I thought—delusion and a strong desire to fuck shit up.

My mother's fractured upbringing of being placed in foster care as a baby meant she had no knowledge of our whakapapa—our history, genealogy—so I had no way of knowing which iwi we belonged to. I sometimes wondered if that was why I was so desperate for a sense of belonging, needy to find a nest to call my own. Whatever the reason, I had certainly gone to extreme measures with Jockey to find some security and a sense of connection. I still intended to honour the contract, but I worried if it may have been a kneejerk reaction to Gavin's new relationship.

"You did the right thing," I assured myself as I turned into the lookout's carpark. "You can't compete with a woman who's willing to lick his ass."

Thankfully the carpark was empty and I was able to park in the best spot that gave me a view of Moa Hill and the glimmering Pacific Ocean.

Staring out at the horizon, the blue sky stretched away forever. It was so clear I imagined I could almost see the deep blue edge of space.

The purity of my surroundings felt polluted when I stepped out of the vehicle with my cock dangling out the open fly of my jeans. Using my phone, I recorded a close-up shot of my flaccid member before lifting the phone and panning out to capture the stunning view of Moa Hill below. The cool breeze nipped at my dick, reminding me of how exposed I was.

I sent Jockey the video with a short message attached: *Your faggots cock out in the wild.*

While I still wasn't crazy about that word I figured Jockey would get a kick out of seeing me refer to myself as a faggot. It was easier to do via text than in person, and showed the sort of respect and obedience he now expected from me.

Finally, I put my cock away and took the chance to enjoy the view without fear of someone busting me balls to the wind. Something about being high above my town made me feel God-like, almighty and in charge. I made a mental note to enjoy the feeling because in just a matter of days I'd be feeling anything but in charge. I wouldn't even be in control of what clothes I wore, or when I could come. It would all be in Jockey's hands.

One of the things that comforted me about becoming Jockey's faggot was how serious he appeared to take the responsibility. The contract outlined in great detail what was expected of me but also of what would be expected of him. As the alpha male he had a responsibility to look after his faggot and make sure I was provided for. He had also been brutally honest with me last night when he'd explained he would never love me like a boyfriend. Yeah, that had hurt, but the pain had been numbed by him telling me he would always remain loyal to me.

Alone on the lookout, listening to the cicadas and native birds, I thought about Jockey's cute ass. I'd got a good look again at it last night and could confidently say he had the sexiest ass I had ever seen. Admittedly, I hadn't seen that many in person but I'd had enough pervy glimpses in locker rooms through the years to know that Jockey's toned little tush reigned supreme. It was high, tambourine-tight and small. I didn't even mind that it was a little hairy. It would still be perfect for fucking.

"Fuuuuck," I groaned, knowing it was pointless to fantasise about my friend in the one way I could never have him. Jockey's views on anal sex were narrow-minded to say the least, but I had to respect them, which meant accepting the only time I'd be allowed near his ass would be to dig my heels into his rump while he fucked me on my back.

Hardly a bad thing considering how much you love being fucked by him.

That whisper of truth was hard to ignore, and perhaps the one that I found most confusing. I had never viewed myself as sexually submissive but the proof was in the fucking; Jockey had bitched me out twice now and I'd loved every second of it. The other odd thing was that aside from his ass, which I'd been checking out for years, I can't say he had ever made me turn my head the way good boy Brian had. But there was something in the greasy way Jockey moved, those badly-drawn tattoos on his shoulders, the nastiness of his fuck-sneer...they came together in an overpowering sexual frenzy that had me now craving his cock.

If I thought about it, *really* thought about it, our new dynamic said more about Jockey's ability to dominate than me being a superfan of the bottom bunk. Because I was pretty sure I wouldn't have signed a contract like this with just anyone. It had to be with someone I could trust, someone I respected enough to submit to, and someone who could fuck me to paradise.

After years of dismissing the scruffy stoner as a slapstick version of masculinity, I now knew Jockey Savage had the goods to back up his claims of alphahood. Those who had not experienced the power of Jockey's thudding hips, or had not laid eyes on his girthy seven inches, would have been clueless to his ability to dominate and destroy. Most people in this town considered him a joke, just like I always had. But that walking joke was now my alpha. My owner. My purpose. And I would honour him and the contract to the best of my ability.

The serenity of my surrounding was suddenly disturbed by the chirping of my phone receiving a text message.

Jockey: You can come to my place now for the inspection. And make sure you are naked when you knock on the door.

Mike: R u being serious????

Jockey: I think you know the answer to that.

He knew as well as I did that the contract didn't start until next Friday, which meant I was under no obligation to follow his orders until then. Knowing this, I dared to push back a little.

Mike: What's in it for me?

Jockey: The pleasure of a real man's company.

Mike: Do you have a friend over?

Jockey: Cheeky bitch.

Mike: LOL

Jockey: If you don't turn up naked then I guess you'll miss out on this.

A picture then filled the message box: a semi-erect cock hovering above two low-hanging balls. Apparently Jockey thought all he had to do was tug the elastic of his pants down, snap a picture, and I'd come running.

I stared at the image, fingers hovering over the screen, but I ultimately put my phone away without typing back. There was no point in replying. We both knew what my answer would be.

Chapter 3

LIFE WAS STRANGE.

If you'd asked me a couple of months ago whether I'd be standing naked outside Jockey's sleepout in broad daylight, I'd have thought you were kidding. But here I was knocking at his door in just my birthday suit. Thankfully the door to his sleepout was hidden from the street thanks to the camelia bush running along the fence, but I was still at risk of being spotted by his aunt and uncle whose house was only a few metres away.

My clothes were tucked in a neat pile just off to the side; easily within reach just in case I had to make a run to the car in a hurry. The fear of being busted had forced my dick to flaccid territory and my nuts felt like a pair of shrivelled raisins. I could hear Jockey moving about inside the sleepout but he didn't appear to be making a move towards the door. Worried he'd not heard the first knock, I banged on the door a second time, desperate to get inside.

"Won't be a moment," he hollered.

That moment turned out to be nearly two minutes before the piss-taking prick finally opened the door. Smiling as he stood in the doorway, he looked me up and down, concentrating on the droop of my soft dick. "What a good boy. You did what you were told."

I might have been his faggot but I wasn't a vampire so I didn't wait for an invite before pushing past him to go inside. Jockey laughed at my rushed entry, giving my ass a playful slap as I went by. He then bent down and picked up my clothes for me and took them over to the couch where he sat down

Aside from being barefoot, Jockey was fully clothed in a white t-shirt and one of the many pairs of camo pants he owned. This only heightened my sense of nakedness. I stood stiffly in the centre of the room—unyielding, unmoving, and painfully unsexy—while my eyes darted about. I let out a groan when I saw what was hanging above his bed.

Tied to the headboard were the Calvin Kleins I'd gifted him. The ones I had worn the night I lost my virginity. Seeing them hung up like a victor's flag made my sphincter clench. Not helping matters was how he'd turned them inside out with the ass-end on full display. Dried and crusty semen clung to the material, discoloured and grotesque.

Jockey smiled when he saw what I was staring at. "Do you like what I've done with your knickers?"

"No. It's embarrassing."

"Aw, don't be embarrassed. You should be proud."

I couldn't tell if he was being serious or taking the piss. Regardless I was still embarrassed. Which I'm sure he could tell, and probably enjoyed. He spread his legs and pointed to the carpet between his feet. "Sit down. Knees bent and legs open."

I obeyed, assuming the position. If I were clothed then it would have felt like a natural position, casually male and at ease. But naked I felt anything but at ease, my balls and cock on full display for his viewing pleasure.

The silence that followed only seemed to reinforce our roles; Jockey the king and me his lowly servant. I lowered my gaze to his feet. They were skinny and pale, a little hairy. He shifted, flexing his ankle absently, and the motion fascinated me. In less than a week's time he would have the power to make me kiss those feet, worship them. He could have me lie on the ground and use my face as a footstool. Anything. And if I protested—perhaps even if I only bored him—there would be consequences.

It doesn't matter. It's what you deserve. And really, Mike, it's what you want.

"Sorry about those, dog," I heard him say.

I glanced up and saw the sexy hint of a smile. He pointed at my chest.

"I didn't realise how much root rash I gave you last night," he said. "Looks like I might have got a bit carried away again."

"It's okay. At least their below my neckline this time."

Despite his apology, Jockey seemed pleased with the work of his sharp teeth—though his voice was pancake flat when he said, "They suit you. Make you look like a slut."

"I'm sure that's what Gavin thought too when he saw them this morning."

"The G-man saw them, did he? Did he say anything?"

"Did he what. He's under the impression I have a new girlfriend and he wouldn't stop going on and fucking on about using a condom so I don't get her pregnant."

"You should have just told him it's your pussy getting banged. That way he won't have to worry about anyone getting knocked up."

While Jockey laughed at his own bad joke, I wondered seriously if it were time to say something to Gavin about my sexuality. It had never felt a pressing issue before on account of my lack of action with either gender. But things were different now.

"Do you think maybe I should tell him?" I asked Jockey. "About me being into guys, I mean."

"That's up to you."

"Maybe I should. At least then he might stop asking me about the sexy vampire."

Jockey threw me a questioning look. "Who's the sexy vampire?"

"Take a guess," I said, pointing to the lovebites on my chest.

He smiled, his eyes lighting up, but he didn't quite laugh. "That's brilliant. The sexy vampire. I like it."

"I don't because now Gavin is asking me to introduce him to this imaginary girlfriend of mine. This morning he even suggested I invite the sexy vampire over for dinner one night."

"Then why don't you? I'm not going to turn down a free feed."

"You want me to introduce you as the sexy vampire?"

"I was thinking more along the lines of you introducing me as the man who fucks you. If he has any questions about our arrangement I can help you answer them."

"You can't be serious?"

"Why wouldn't I be serious? I'd quite like to tell the guy banging my ex-girlfriend that I'm now fucking his stepson's ass."

"You told me you didn't care about Gavin dating Fiona."

"I don't. But I'd still enjoy telling him all about how tight your pussy is."

"You're such a fucking weirdo," I said as if this were pre-contract times. Realising my mistake, I quickly apologised. "Fuck. Sorry. I'm sorry, sir. I didn't mean to swear at you."

Jockey dismissed my concern with a wave of his hand. "It's all good, Mike. We can still banter like mates. Just because you're my faggot doesn't change that. If you ever need to apologise for anything I'll let you know. Otherwise just try your best to act normal."

"Thanks...but it's sort of hard to act normal while I'm sat here naked."

"You'll have to get used to it because you'll be naked around me most of the time moving forward."

"Will I?"

"Yep. I want easy access to that ass of yours for whenever I get horny." He shifted his foot to between my legs and very gently nudged my balls, his toes cool against the heat of my sac. "That's gonna be the best thing about having my own faggot. Fucking you whenever I feel like it. I reckon I'll be giving you five or six loads a day when we first start."

"Ouch."

"You'll be fine." His toes curled around my dick, squeezing like fingers. After three gentle squeezes, his toes released their grip and he pulled his foot back. "So what's your plan of attack for the next seven days?"

"Plan of attack?"

"Who do you plan on screwing before the contract starts."

"No one. Well, aside from you, of course."

"Is that wise?"

"Are you saying you want me to fuck around?"

"I'm just saying that you'd be stupid not to make the most of these next seven days. Once Friday rolls around there will be no more fucking whoever you please and no wanking to your heart's content. When the contract starts I will own those sexy balls of yours and the cum they brew."

"I hear what you're saying but I don't think I'm the casual hookup sort of person."

"What about the blowjob you gave to some dude in the park?"

"That was a one-off."

He stared straight into my eyes, his brows in a conspiratorial arch. I worried he was about to start quizzing me about the blowjob, maybe clarify which park it took place at, demand to know more about the cock I'd swallowed a load from...

"Then all the more reason to play the field while you can," he finally said, sparing me the chore of fabricating some made-up story. "But if you are going to screw around then make sure you play safe. No bareback."

"You sound like Gavin."

"No, I sound smart. I plan on fucking you raw all year and I'd rather not worry about my faggot leaving me pissing razor blades."

"Honestly, Jockey, it's not something you have to worry about. It's highly unlikely I'm gonna meet anyone before Friday."

In an abrupt end to the conversation, he slid off the couch and walked past me to go lay down on the bed. He didn't even look at me when he next spoke: "Take yourself into the bathroom and have a shower. I want that pussy of yours squeaky clean for the inspection."

TEN MINUTES LATER, I emerged from the misty bathroom with a towel wrapped around my waist, eager to see if sex would follow my inspection. Jockey was still lying on his bed, but he'd stripped down to just his cheap satin boxers. One arm was up over his head, showing his pit—the other was looking at his phone—at least I thought it was his phone. It looked a lot like mine.

It is mine!

"What the fuck are you doing with my phone?".

"Don't mind me," he said, not taking his eyes off the screen. "I was just taking a look at the sort of porn you like to watch."

I wanted to throttle him but I feared the consequences come Friday. Forcing myself to remain calm, I patiently waited for him to finish snooping. It helped that he was half-naked. How could I be angry at such a sexy sight? Those sinewy muscles of his. The long, hairy legs I wished I could lick the length of. The lightly tented crotch of his boxers...it was all serving delicious eye candy.

"Are you into being tied up?" he asked. "Cause there's a fuck tonne of BDSM porn on here."

"Uh..."

"Uh...what? It's a simple question."

"I like the idea of tying someone else up...and sort of, um, taking control."

He met my gaze and grinned, a slick and slimy spreading of his lips. "Interesting."

That's all he said before putting my phone down and ordering me to ditch the towel.

I resisted obeying for a moment, long enough to blink and breathe, then dropped the towel to the floor. Once again I was stood before him naked, his plaything, his obedient bitch.

Jockey fetched a measuring tape from his bedside drawer then came towards me, backing me up against the wall. That sexy mouth of his hovered just inches from mine. Then, he leaned even closer, his lips a hairsbreadth away, his breath caressing my face. Desire flickered in my balls and I thought he was going to kiss me.

Spoiler alert: he didn't.

"Time to see if you were telling the truth in the contract," he said, crouching to the floor and sticking the end of the measuring tape by my feet.

"I'm hardly going to lie about my height."

He looked up at me, his hot breath blowing over my naked balls. "It never hurts to doublecheck."

He slowly raised up, extending the tape up the wall until I felt his fingers brushing the top of my head. "Five foot ten," he mumbled to himself.

"I told you so."

Ignoring me, Jockey went and collected a pen and piece of paper from the same drawer the measuring tape had been in and wrote down: *5 ft 10. Faggot was honest.*

This was such a waste of time, I thought, but Jockey continued with what turned out to be an intense examination. He checked my shoe size, measured my waist and chest, jabbed fingers in my mouth to inspect my teeth and gums, checked the amount of hair under my arms, and even fingered my asshole to test its tightness. I'd tried not to laugh when I saw him write down the very scientific description of *tight as fuck.*

Accompanying the invasive inspection was his phone recording every inch of my body, no doubt to go with the photos he already possessed. It should have worried me, his growing collection of intimate pictures and video, but I was too lost in the way he gazed upon me, making me feel sexy and wanted.

After he had finished examining my balls—gripping and jostling them in the palm of his hand before listing them down in the contract as being of *average size*—I was ordered to lay down on the floor and get myself hard.

That wouldn't take much. I was already half-hard by the time he'd finished molesting my balls.

Laid naked on the floor, the manky carpet scratching my back, I began to masturbate in front of him. Jockey watched me, hooded amber eyes flicking from my face to my groin, where my hand squeezed and pulled at my manhood. The feel of his gaze on me, unshifting and obvious, was turning me on. Which only made me want to jerk harder, faster.

"Let go of your cock," he said sharply. "It's not gonna get any bigger than that."

I wished I could have argued with him but the fact my slit was leaking dick dew was proof he was correct. He lined the tape against my shaft. First he measured along the top and then beneath before writing the answer down in the contract.

"See," I said. "Six inches."

"It's not actually." He turned the piece of paper around to show me what he'd written down:

The faggot has a small dick. Five inches.

"Five inches?" I squawked. "That's wrong."

"Measuring tapes don't lie, Mike."

"That one is." I went to sit up but he pressed a hand to my chest and forced me to lay back down.

"If you want to get technical about it then your dick is five-point-seven inches fully erect."

"Yeah, which is practically six inches. You round up."

"Real men round up, not faggots. Faggots must round down, which means your dick is only five inches long. And because your dick is only five inches, it means I have to list you down as having a small dick."

"It's not small though." I glanced down at my offended appendage. "Is it?"

"What's it matter? I still think it's sexy."

"It matters to me."

"Who cares if you're underhung. Loads of guys have tiny cocks."

"So you think I'm tiny?"

"I don't care how big or small your dick is." I couldn't miss the small snicker he barely tried to hide. "As a faggot it's your pussy you should be taking pride in."

"I'm asking if *you* think it's small?"

"Yes, Mike. I think it's small." He grabbed hold of my cock, squeezing lightly, halfway between threat and promise. "You have a small dick. And that's okay." He then said it again, much more softly, like he was performing ASMR, "*You have a small dick. And that's okay.*"

I wanted to tell him to go fuck himself but I was too embarrassed to speak. It didn't help knowing that inside his pants was a dick that put mine to shame.

"Are you mad at me?" he asked, still squeezing my shaft.

"No," I lied. "I'm just embarrassed."

"Of course you are." His eyes briefly met mine before going to my crotch. "Who wouldn't be embarrassed by this inadequate thing."

"Inadequate!?"

"I'm not saying it to me mean, I'm saying it because it's best you be honest with yourself. And with me." He let go of my dick and placed his hand on my thigh, his head dipping towards my crotch as if he were talking to my dick instead. "Now, I want you to repeat after me 'My name is Michael Freeman and I have small dick.'"

I shook my head.

"Michael, you need to say this." Jockey's breath was so warm on my crotch and, despite being huffy and humiliated, it sent pleasure shooting down to my yearning cock. "You're not doing yourself any favours by living in denial about it."

"I'm not saying it."

"Yes you are." He gripped my cock again, giving it a slow tug. "My name is Michael Freeman and I have a small dick. That's all you have to say. Admit it to yourself, and to me."

"Fuck," I whispered under my breath, torn between the pleasure of his hand and the cruelty of his words.

"Say it, baby. You'll feel so much better."

"My name..." I swallowed. "My name is Michael Freeman and I have a small dick."

"Good boy. And again."

"My name is Michael Freeman and I have a small dick."

"Keep going."

"My name is Michael Freeman and I have a small dick. My name is Michael Freeman and I have a small dick. My name is Michael Freeman and I have a small dick."

Over and over I said what Jockey wanted to hear, telling him, telling myself, telling the world that I was the owner of a small cock. The more I said it the more he pleasured my dick with his hand. I'd never been so fucking aroused, or so fucking hard, or so fucking humiliated, in my life.

"Louder," Jockey whispered, kissing the tip of my leaking piss slit.

His mouth suddenly slurped over the head of my cock and I found myself chanting the humiliating mantra with more passion, more force, more volume: "MY NAME IS MICAEL FREEMAN AND I HAVE A SMALL DICK! MY NAME IS MICHAEL FREEMAN AND I HAVE A SMALL DICK!"

The louder I spoke, the harder Jockey sucked my dick. His fingers tickled my taint while his tongue did magical things to my shaft, as if he were rewarding me for this emasculating mindfuck.

I felt tears bleeding down my cheeks as the words cut like a knife through my male pride, ripping my confidence to shreds. At some point I went from feeling like I was following an order to making a confession. And that's when my voice cracked as my dick ejaculated inside Jockey's mouth.

Through panting moans I continued acknowledging my lack of size, "My name is Michael Freeman and I have a small dick. My name is Michael Freeman and I have a small dick." It only stopped when Jockey's face closed in on mine. One of his hands found my balls. His other grabbed the back of my head and pulled me in for a kiss.

Our mouths opened and Jockey's tongue rolled onto mine. A wad of bitter film spilled into my mouth.

My eyes widened. I knew what it was. Jockey's tongue swirled and his lips opened and closed again and again. The ball of my cum seemed to grow and build until fluid leaked from our faces. It was disgusting. It was vile. It was fucking beautiful.

I shut my eyes and wound my tongue around Jockey's, tasting the thickness that filled our kiss. A streak of milky fluid poured down my face.

Jockey slowly pulled away. "Feel better?"

I nodded timidly. And in a weird way I did feel better. A little bit broken, but better.

"I can't wait for Friday," he said. "I'm gonna take such good care of my faggot and his sexy little dick."

Jockey's words could have been conceived as both a comfort and a threat. In this particular instance, the comfort to the words was the threat. Knowing I was just days away from being considered his personal property shouldn't have made me feel good and cared for. But it did. It really fucking did.

Chapter 4

WHEN I ARRIVED BACK home, I discovered Gavin and Fiona sat on the back deck drinking fizzy wine from plastic flute glasses. Judging by their flushed faces, and the nearly empty bottle on the garden table, they weren't on their first glass. Gavin had unzipped the overalls he had on, allowing the blue material to slip from his broad, brown shoulders and expose him from the waist up. His hairy chest was soaked with sweat, indicating he'd either been working on Betsy, or maybe Fiona.

"Mikey." Gavin spoke louder than usual. "You're home early."

I couldn't tell if this was him acting or if he'd forgotten I had said I would be home at two o'clock. "Yeah," I said. "Home early."

"Hello, Michael," Fiona said, kind of fake-polite, like she was really forcing it.

I glanced around for any sign of the third party, curious to see who the man was Fiona had chosen for the pair's threeway. While Fiona was distracted looking inside her handbag for her cigarettes, Gavin shot me a discreet wink and pointed is head in the direction of Betsy.

He can't have been as drunk as I thought since he clearly knew who I was looking for. Turning around, I looked in the direction his head had pointed. From underneath Betsy protruded a pair of denim-clad legs, and I heard the unmistakable sound of someone applying a wrench with great force to an unyielding piece of metal.

"Goddamn son of a bitch," the owner of the legs said forcefully.

"Monkey man," Gavin hollered, "come out from the belly of that beast and show yourself."

Monkey man's feet scuffed at the dirt as he slid out from beneath the bus. The legs gave way to a naked torso, the skin golden from hours spent in the sun. This in turn was followed by a youthful face that was more boy than man. It was also a face that I recognised in a heart-squeezing instant.

The blond-haired youth squinted, covering his eyes with one hand to block out the sun.

"What's up?" the boy puffed.

"Come meet Mike," Gavin said, sounding, I thought, slightly bossy.

The youth pushed himself to his feet and faced us. The light jolt of his body and panicky pupils—only obvious if you were looking for signs of fear—told me he recognised me too. Quickly hiding his unease, he wandered over and joined us on the deck.

"Hey," he said, gazing at me with a guarded expression.

Clearing his throat, Gavin said, "Mike, I want you to meet Stryder. Stryder, this is Mike."

The fright I'd seen mirrored in the boy's eyes had already been replaced with a mask of cocky contempt. I imagined it was the sort of look he gave his customers at Hickford park.

"*Mike* and I have met before." Stryder half-smiled, half-sneered, his top lip curling upward while the edges of his mouth drooped "At that party, remember?"

I nodded, choked out a, "That's right," and swallowed afterwards. The Kentucky Derby was in my chest.

"What party?" Gavin asked.

"Just some party," I said, going along with Stryder's lie. "I can't remember whose."

"It was Rowan's party," Stryder said. He came to stand next to me, closer than I would have liked. His mussed hair and sweaty brow reminded me of more interesting things. "The three of us got chatting in the bathroom, remember?"

At first I thought Stryder was trying to give me a panic attack on purpose the way he was recycling bits of the truth, but when I saw the clueless look in his blue eyes I realised he probably thought he was spinning a believable yarn. *Fucking idiot.*

"Whose Rowan?" Gavin asked. "I don't think I've met this friend."

I chuckled, buying time, but all I could come up with was, "Just some guy."

"Some guy who?" Gavin sounded suspicious.

Stryder looked at me.

I looked at Stryder.

Gavin looked at both of us. Waiting...

Sweat began collecting in my armpits. I opened my mouth, but nothing came out.

Just as the lack of a response was about to become awkward, Fiona saved my bacon by pulling out a cigarette and saying to Gavin, "Spark me up, babe."

Like the pussy-whipped bitch that he was, Gavin eagerly snatched up the red lighter from the table and cupped a hand around the top of it as he leaned over and lit her cigarette.

I untensed, just a fraction.

Fiona exhaled a satisfied plume of grey smoke and sat back in her chair. "Gavin tells me you've got yourself a girlfriend. Who's the lucky lady?"

Oh shit... I'd already told Gavin some fake name for my mystery vampire but I couldn't remember what name I'd used. "Georgia?" It came out more like a question than an answer.

Gavin didn't say anything so either I'd guessed right or he hadn't been paying attention the last time.

"Georgia," Fiona said back to me, sounding as if she was using the name as mouthwash. "That's a pretty name."

"Yeah."

"Matthew will be jealous," Fiona said, smiling in a way that made me worry how much she knew.

"W-Why would he be jealous?" I stammered.

"Because you will be busy spending all your time with your new girlfriend and not him." Fiona exhaled another cloud of smoke. "I know how territorial he is of you. Matthew is always going on about how much he enjoys spending time with you."

"Everybody enjoys spending time with, Mikey," Gavin said, only half taking the piss. "He learned how to be fun from me, you know?"

Fiona chuckled. "Did he now?"

Gavin and Fiona fell into their usual routine of flirty innuendo, allowing Stryder and I to stand there quietly while we both no doubt wished we could be somewhere else. Each time I glanced over at the boy I would find his eyes looking at me, sending me silent whispers of *don't say a fucking word.* He needn't have worried. The last thing I wanted was to have people know I'd witness intergenerational bum play at Hickford Park.

Without the bathroom stall in the way, I was able to get a proper look at him and gauge how attractive he was. Yes, he was a very good-looking boy, and those naturally pale pink lips of his would look heavenly wrapped around a cock. But on closer inspection there was a sharpness in his face, a world-weariness in his eyes, something that took away some of his angelic allure.

Rather than stay outside battling through an awkward interaction, I excused myself and went inside to sit in the lounge. I could not believe that the boy whose ass I'd seen feasted upon by Mr Quayle was to be the *man* Gavin had sex with. I also couldn't believe the young idiot had been using his real name while hustling. That meant he was either naive or stupid. But remembering how well-fucked Stryder's asshole had looked my guess was it was a case of stupidity.

There was no way I could let Gavin go through with this threeway. Not if it meant he was going to get humped by a teenage hustler who had let a man old enough to be his grandfather lick his ass for a lousy twenty bucks.

But what could I do?

It wasn't like I could tell Gavin about what I had seen, and I doubted very much if he would appreciate me trying to talk him out of it. Gavin's mind had been made up and he was determined to give Fiona what she wanted.

Twenty minutes later, right after Fiona and Stryder left, Gavin wandered inside with a guilty smirk on his face. He didn't say anything at first, just sat himself down beside me on the couch while giving me furtive glances. Our roles suddenly felt reversed; me the parental figure and him the idiot teen looking for approval.

Finally, Gavin asked, "So what do you think?"

"What do you think is the more important question?"

"Honestly, I'm impressed. I was expecting some crusty old bugger but Stryder's a fit young lad. If I was gay I'd probably marry the sexy bugger." After a small chuckle came a twinge of doubt in his voice. "I'm not sure about the logistics of the whole butt sex thing though. I'm not really all that ass-aware: it's just there, it does its thing, and it gets washed in the shower with the rest of me. So far it's all been one-way, though."

"But you're going to let Stryder make it two-way?"

"Maybe." Gavin gave me a little smile when he said it, but it was a wary one. "Ordinarily I'd be like 'hell no' but my spidey senses are telling me to give it a shot. Live a little."

"Your spidey senses are crazy. I can't believe you're actually going to let him fuck you."

"It's not that much of a big deal."

Judging by the redness creeping over his cheeks, that wasn't entirely true. And when he abruptly got and scampered back outside it was clear the topic wasn't up for discussion.

Chapter 5

IN AN IDEAL WORLD, Sunday would be a relaxed day. A gentle end to the weekend. My cock's schedule, though, clearly hadn't got that memo. I awoke with a raging hard-on that demanded attention. After meeting its demands, resulting in a wet stomach I had to wipe up with a dirty sock, I rolled out of bed and went on autopilot as I got dressed and made my way to the kitchen to make myself some breakfast.

The house was quiet as I knew it would be. Gavin had told me last night his plans to get up early so he could go play happy families with Fiona and her children, joining them on a family outing to the zoo. His enthusiasm to play the role of fun dad to Fiona's children still left me a bag of bitter bones but at least now I wasn't so scared of the inevitable; being asked to move out. Signing Jockey's contract had rescued me from the worst fate of all: being abandoned. So while becoming another man's owned faggot wasn't ideal it had at least bought me some time. When Gavin finally asked me to move out, and he would at some point, I would now have Jockey to run to.

After downing a cup of sugary black coffee—which reminded me I'd have to buy milk at some point today—and two bits of toast smothered in Marmite, I returned to my bedroom and switched on my laptop. I had hoped to spend the day writing more of my novel but before doing that I decided to look up the websites Jockey had written down for me to research. I knew he would quiz me on them come next Friday so it was wise to have at least give them a quick read-through.

The website at the top of the list was called The Hierarchy. As soon as the landing page came up with its black background and red font, I realised that this would not be a quick read-through like I had hoped. There was a menu bar with oodles of links and articles explaining the ins and outs of being a faggot. Apparently there were lots of men like Jockey who were into this sort of thing. Men who considered themselves alpha males and who expected to be worshipped by lesser men such as myself.

This shit is intense!

I had been well aware the contract I had signed was serious. Jockey had made that very clear in the terms and conditions. But what I had not expected was just how much of a subculture there was with this sort of dynamic. What we had was hardly unique if what I was reading on his website was true. It wasn't as though I had never heard of master/slave dynamics in a sexual sense but I had always assumed it was a bit of kink people kept inside the bedroom. That did not appear to be the case with the men posting on this website.

I clicked on a video buried amongst the words on the screen, and I flinched in shock when it started playing a scene mid-fuck of a beefy bear pounding the shit out of some skinny twink's asshole. Wincing in sympathy for the bottom, I watched as the top dished out a sadistic and ruthless fuck. The twink was wailing, a warbled mix of pain and pleasure, until his dominant lover slapped his face and told him to shut the fuck up.

Written beneath the video was a description that was both heartless and uncomfortably accurate:

Simply put, this is what it's really like when an Alpha gets a faggot in a room and takes what he wants. This isn't studio porn sex. This is a dominant predator breeding an inferior animal. #HierarchyIsTruth!

Despite my pangs of sympathy for the boy being rutted, I found myself getting turned on by the video. But I wasn't picturing myself as the bitched-out bottom, I was picturing myself as the alpha male taking what he wanted. Although I had yet to ever penetrate another man's asshole, I had always assumed that would be my preference. Unfortunately that was not the role I'd been assigned with Jockey. The lanky stoner was my alpha and I his inferior animal. Just that term alone was enough to piss me off, but being angry only made me more hot and bothered as I watched the video through to the alpha's climax.

Finished with the video, I scrolled down where I read more sadistic spiels of what the website labelled sexual truth:

ALPHAS RULE THE WORLD. Faggots are the possessions of their Kingdom. A King doesn't need to ask to take something he owns already!

Alphas speak with their bodies. Faggots obey every word!

True faggots are always wrong. Even if you are factually correct about something, you are wrong. Practice saying "Sorry, Sir" as many times in each conversation as possible.

New fags think that being a faggot is about being fucked and used sexually. Being a true fag is a mindset, a lifestyle, a

realization of your inferiority. Being a fag is who you are; being a hole for men to use is just one of your many duties.

ON AND ON THE COMMENTS and commandments went, making it very clear that as a faggot your role and purpose in life was to give your alpha pleasure and make his life easier. The most infuriating part was that on some level I understood the bullshit reasoning behind this; making the alpha's life easier would also make the faggot's life easier. And although it rattled me to think I was merely a servant, I could not deny that I liked the thought of Jockey protecting me and taking care of life's bigger decisions on my behalf.

But do I want to be treated like a hole?

The answer to that was no but I had already signed the contract. I had given Jockey my word and unless I could come up with two grand—the price to buy my freedom—then I knew I'd just have to make the best of it. This was typical of me though; making a decision and then constantly questioning if it were the right one. Thankfully, or unthankfully, I was wasting my time stressing about it because starting on Friday I would be embarking on a twelve month journey that would see me as Jockey's living, breathing possession.

Clicking out of The Hierarchy website, I brought up a new page and typed in the next web address Jockey had recommended I check out. Some site called Moa Hill Secrets.

Although the web address was for Moa Hill Secrets, the name on the landing page was Hickford Homos.

"Oh shit," I whispered when I realised what the website was about.

This was the new site to host all the Hickford Homo pictures and videos that had been taken down after the story of some homophobe vigilante filming gay men cruising had made the local news two years ago. The original site had caused quite the sensation at the time and had ruined several marriages of closetcase men who'd been caught on camera getting their rocks off. One boy at school, Isaac Fraser, was one of the unlucky sods to find his face on the website and it had made his life at school a living hell. What had made Isaac's case even more scandalous was no one had suspected he might be gay. The stocky Isaac had been one of the more popular boys at my school where he was a member of the school's first fifteen rugby team. Overnight Isaac's popularity took a dive to the bottom of the barrel and he'd been mocked endlessly about appearing on the website until eventually dropping out of school. The last I heard he'd moved to Auckland in the hope of escaping his sullied reputation.

While someone like Isaac coming out as gay was never going to be a walk in the park—no pun intended—it wasn't his love of dick that caused the most damage to his reputation. It was that snarky term the site had coined—Hickford Homos—that was so damn toxic. Perhaps it was the alliteration, the way the phrase rolled off the tongue, but those two words packed a punch and were filled with a lot of meaning. It had less to do with being gay and more to do with the insinuation of being dirty, slutty, unclean...a joke.

One of the old coot journalists who worked for the local newspaper at the time had written an opinion piece arguing that the shame inflicted on Hickford Homos was a sign of progress that gay men were being held to the same social standards as straight people. He'd tried to back his ridiculous point up by referring to some Moa Hill sex scandal from the 1950s when a group of 'wayward and immoral' school girls became known as the Sawmill Madams when it was discovered they were prostituting on weekends at the site of an abandoned sawmill.

Many people my age probably assumed the Sawmill Madams were an urban legend—the phrase *'she's nothing but a Sawmill Madam'* was still used as an insult for promiscuity in certain circles—but being the history geek that I am I'd looked up the case years ago so I knew that the journalist had been referring to a very real incident. What he had failed to mention in his article was that very few of the men who'd frequented the sawmill had suffered any damage to their reputations. But each of those school girls wound up being plagued for decades by nasty whispers behind their back, their reputations permanently damaged. So while nearly seventy years may have separated the two scandals there was still a similar backlash for those who stepped out of line of society's norms. And apparently getting dicked at night in a seedy park qualified.

I had purposely avoided looking online for the Hickford Homo videos at the time, telling anyone who would listen that it just fed into a culture of hate and that we needed to rise above the *I'm-not-dirty-like-you* bullshit. My moral high horse did little to convince my friends not to visit the website though. Both Jockey and Brian had allowed their curiosity to get the better of them and each told me later about what they had seen. The naturally conservative Brian had been left disturbed by the videos, unable to believe why men would want to do something so "gross" and in "such a dirty place." In contrast Jockey had found the videos hilarious and had admitted to watching Isaac's video on repeat because he liked the noises the young rugby player had made. In hindsight I should have read more into but at the time I'd just put it down to Jockey's naturally sex-obsessed personality.

At the top of the page was a small intro giving some background to the website's content followed by instructions on how you could upload pictures and videos of your own if they were of men getting it on at Hickford Park. I instantly thought about my contract with Jockey and how it had said I had to choose between getting a tattoo baring his name or allow him to film me getting fucked at Hickford Park and then have the video uploaded online. Clearly this was the website such a video would end up on.

My stomach felt sick at the thought.

While I was morally opposed to visiting this website, I decided it would be wise to check some of the content out since there was the very real possibility my ass could end up on here. Don't get me wrong, I didn't want to wind up on here but I also wasn't too keen on being permanently inked with Jockey's name somewhere on my body.

A cold shiver tapped my spine as I appreciated just how dark and sadistic that part of the contract was. In stark contrast to my fear was a spike of arousal zinging around my dick. As disgusted as I was with myself I could not deny that some secret part of me found Jockey's sadistic demands a turn-on. That was the fucked-up part.

I started scrolling through the mosaic of images, most of them photos, until I found what I was looking for. The video of Isaac Fraser. It was relatively easy to find because the thumbnail was a closeup of his young, handsome face; his mop of brown hair with its bleached-blond tips stuck out like dog's balls.

Without even thinking, I got up and locked my bedroom door and pulled the curtains before returning to sit in front of the laptop. I knew I was alone in the house, but my heart was hammering, my hands jittered, and the idea of someone walking in and seeing anything made me want to vomit.

I clicked play.

The video started with a shot of Isaac and an older guy walking towards the camera. Judging by the brightness of the sky it was either late afternoon or an early summer evening. Dressed in skimpy rugby shorts and a singlet, Isaac looked as though he'd come straight from rugby practice. He walked with the same cocky strut I'd seen him do many times at school; the sort of walk that said *I'm the man*.

The older guy walking beside him was thin and looked to be in his mid-to-late thirties. He was tall and pale with a shaved head and nasty eyes. His nose skewed crooked on his face, and his cauliflower ears gave him the look of an ugly brute, the sort of guy who broke legs for a living. His gaunt face also gave the impression meth was a regular part of his diet. To be honest, the dude looked like a skinhead. A drug-fucked skinhead. He seemed greasy, slimy, smarmy and dangerous. If that's who Isaac was about to have sex with then I questioned the young rugby player's taste in men. But then maybe he liked the bad boy types, even if they were on the mature side and lacking in the looks department.

It took me a moment to get my bearings with where they were. They were on the grassy field of Hickford Park and headed in the direction of a far corner of the field where if my memory served correct they would soon enter a small row of trees—which I assumed was where the guy filming was hidden.

The image became shaky as the pair got closer, like the phone being used to film this had been hidden in a hurry. The unsuspecting pair nodded in the direction of whoever was filming; the older dude even asking "You wanna come watch?"

My heart raced a little faster. If this were a horror film then the idiots had just invited their killer to join them.

The person filming didn't respond but must have given a nod or something because the older dude then said, "Well, come on. You can have a turn screwing him after me if you like."

To my surprise, Isaac looked completely unbothered by his older friend offering his ass to a stranger. But judging by the tented front of his rugby shorts he wasn't about to turn down any action.

The film became dark when they made their way through the trees but it soon became bright again when they found their way to a small clearing. I thought the pair would get down to business right away but instead they just stood there as if an invisible wall separated them.

While the older man's gaze flitted about in all directions, Isaac only had eyes for the man's crotch. "I can't believe you're finally going to let me have a turn on it," Isaac said. "I've been trying to get your attention for weeks. My mate told me how big you are."

The skinhead sneered. "Well, today's your lucky day, ain't it?"

"Definitely."

"But you better be sure you're up for it because once my dick is in there I ain't stopping until I nut. Got it?"

"Fine by me," Isaac said confidently. "I've taken big ones before."

"As big as this?" The meth-head unzipped his fly and hauled out a semi-erect cock bigger than mine when fully erect.

Ugly, I thought to myself, feeling a powerful twinge of pure male envy. *Big and ugly*.

Dropping to his knees, Isaac latched his mouth around the unattractive meat that hung from the open fly of the skinhead's crumby jeans. Judging by the initial wince as he dove in it was safe to assume that the porno-sized cock needed a wash. Bad smell or not, it didn't stop Isaac's mouth gliding up and down the man's shaft, cleaning the uncut member with his tongue.

In the darkness of my bedroom, I raked my eyes over Isaac's handsome features affectionately, spellbound by his deepthroating ability. I turned up the volume on the laptop until I could hear the older man's heavy breaths and the sounds of Isaac's sloppy cock slurps.

I was holding my breath, half aroused and half ashamed.

When Isaac finally pulled away to reveal his lover's full size the dick hadn't got any prettier. But the meth-head didn't need a pretty penis. It must have been over eight inches of solid meat hanging out of his pants fly, sheathed in a wrinkled mass of foreskin corrugated with pencil-thick veins. Beneath the hood of skin, the very tip of his plump cockhead was visible, glinting wetly and dribbling a long, suspended thread of milky fluid.

The older man suddenly slapped Isaac's face with his cock and told the boy, "Get ya gear off, bitch."

"I'm only pulling my shorts down."

"Then you don't get the dick," Meth-head replied.

"What?"

"You heard me. Get naked or I'm fucking off. I only root bitches who let me see what I'm fucking. And we both know I can easily find another pig bottom in this park who wants this big dick."

The Isaac I had known at school would have smacked this dude in the face, or at the very least told him to get fucked and then walk away. But then the Isaac at school was also known as a pussy-mad rugby fanatic, not some horny adolescent wanting to get dicked by a drug-fucked skinhead.

Isaac stood there glowering but instead of arguing, or walking away with his pride intact, he let out a resentful sigh and began to take off his shoes. When he removed his socks the camera zoomed in on his pale bare feet, which were smaller and more dainty than I had expected. His singlet came off next, followed by his shorts and tighty-whities that he flicked away with his foot.

My cock stiffened as I took in the intimate details of Isaac's fit physique. Smooth chested with thick, hairy legs, the rugby player was on the stockier side, as was his penis that was short and stubby. He turned around and dropped to his hands and knees, his plump ass appearing just as smooth as his chest.

Mr skinhead looked down at the teen's ass with a sneer of contempt before spitting into the palm of his bony hand which he then wrapped around his big, ugly cock and started lubing his shaft. When he was satisfied with the wetness of his knob, he lowered himself behind his teen lover, lined up the cock with ass, and rammed that thick piece halfway inside Isaac's shitter.

"Arrrgghhh," Isaac cried out.

My ass puckered with phantom pains inside my pants, inside my boxers, like it was imagining how much it must hurt taking something that huge.

But Isaac then let out a low hiss and a very slutty sounding, "Give me that big dick, Daddy!"

Daddy? Did he just call that dude Daddy?

"Fuck me, Daddy! Fuck my boy pussy!"

Apparently I had heard him right the first time. I wanted to laugh at seeing this macho rugby boy begging for a *daddy* to feed his *boy pussy*, but there was nothing funny about Isaac's determination to be fed every inch of that mature meat. He wriggled and writhed on the fat pole, lashing his head about while the ugly-dicked brute skewered the youth's greedy asshole until he'd buried his cock to the hilt.

"That's a pretty loose cunt you got between your legs, boy." The meth-head ground his hips. "You must have started young."

"I'm not loose, Daddy." Isaac glanced over his shoulder at his older lover. "Just experienced."

This made both the cameraman and meth-head laugh. Isaac joined in with their laughter, either unaware they were laughing at him or too damn horny to care.

The laughter came to an abrupt halt when the meth-head spat at Isaac's face. Rather than be horrified like any normal person, Isaac's tongue slipped out and lapped up the nasty prick's spit, and he groaned as if grateful and licked his lips.

This is fucking insane!

The older man shoved Isaac's head forward, making the youth kiss the dirt. He then lowered his own pants some more and hitched up the front of his shirt, exposing a forest of hair down his front. His hard, fuzzy glutes clenched tight every time he impaled the young rugby player.

Isaac began whining, but his dick was a wet iron bar under him and he was jerking it roughly. He almost yelped whenever he arched and took the whole dick inside him—like it hurt, but it hurt weird and good. It was a pitiful noise but one that spoke directly to my balls with how sexy it sounded.

That's the noise Jockey liked. No doubt about it.

Isaac didn't seem to have a problem getting railed hard. He panted and sank even lower to the ground so that his skinhead lover had to follow to stay inside his ass.

"Uh, uh, uh, uh," Isaac uttered on repeat, his head bobbing around from every vicious pump of his lover's hips.

The person filming then walked behind the pair, giving viewers a close-up shot of the older man's hair-covered ass cheeks and his big balls slapping against Isaac's much smaller pair. It was such an invasion of privacy and I couldn't understand how the pair still had not cottoned on to the fact they were being filmed.

And that is when something ominous happened.

The camera came back to give a sideview of the action and raised up so that it captured the older man's smiling face. His beady brown eyes looked straight at the camera as he smiled menacingly. This man knew they were being filmed. He was in on it! He had to be.

My suspicion was confirmed when he said to the dude recording, "Come get a close up of this chewed-up pussy."

Isaac whose face was kissing the dirt must have been too strung out on the man's cock to take any notice of what had been said. While Isaac remained writhing on the ground, babbling on about needing daddy's dick, the camera zoomed in on the anal action, capturing the easy glide of the fat pecker sliding in and out of Isaac's stretched sphincter. I loved the view as the older man fucked him, his ugly cock penetrating Isaac's ass. It turned me on to see it plunge in. It also turned me on watching it withdraw, the hairs around Isaac's asshole, slick with spit, dragging against the veiny shaft.

The person filming finally spoke, his voice young yet husky, "Give it to him, Moose. Make him feel it!"

"That's what I'm doing," the skinhead—apparently named Moose—replied. "Making him feel it."

The person filming retreated a few steps to allow the viewer to see both parties again. They were fucking like dogs, angry and fast on the rough ground, getting close to getting off. Isaac now had scratches on his knees and hands, testimony to just how brutal the force being unleashed on his rectum was. The older dude in back tensed his asscheeks and crammed himself inside.

"Are you ready, slut?" Moose asked Isaac. "Are you ready for Daddy's nut?"

"Yes, Daddy," Isaac whined. "Give me your seed."

As Moose unloaded, his face stretched into a scream, but he made no sound as he tugged Isaac roughly onto the full length of his erection. Without warning he pushed Isaac's face into the ground, holding his hips to keep his ass high, and hammered at it a few times; Isaac growled low and his stubby cock squirted twice, painting the earth with strings of school boy jizz before sliding forward and falling free of the older man's erection behind him.

The guy filming the pair began to laugh—a high-pitched cackle that made me think of loopy hyenas. The camera zoomed in on the rivers of jizz leaking out of Isaac's now gaping asshole, the boy's anal lips struggling in vain to close.

"What are you, bitch?" Moose asked Isaac, giving the boy's rump a slap. "Tell me what you are. You know the rules round here."

The rules?

Isaac took a shuddering breath and spoke, but his voice was so low I couldn't make out what he said.

"Louder," the skinhead demanded, giving Isaac's ass another slap. "I wanna hear you say it. Own that shit, bitch."

Taking another deep breath, Isaac then whispered, "I've been made loose by Moose."

"And again, bitch!"

"I'm loose by Moose. Loose by Moose. Loose by Moose." Isaac kept saying it on repeat. "Loose by Moose. Loose by Moose. Loose by Moose."

There was no denying the statement was accurate. He had indeed been left *loose by Moose*, but it felt unnecessarily cruel to make him say it, like he was having his nose rubbed in his own shit. Unfortunately I knew how Isaac must have felt. Sort of. It reminded me a lot of Jockey making me admit over and over about having a small cock.

"Loose by Moose. Loose by Moose," still chanting the degrading phrase, Isaac turned his head and looked straight at the camera. "Loose by Moose. Loose by—" His mouth dangled open, frozen in shock, eyes wide. "Did-Did you just record us?"

A snarky laugh was the response.

Isaac looked livid and scared at the same time. "You better fucking not have." He got to his feet, looking like he was about to snatch the phone away and that was when the video abruptly ended.

Sat there with a full-on boner in my pants, I felt numb. I had just witnessed a betrayal. An incredibly cruel betrayal. That skinhead bloke named Moose must have known what was happening. Why the fuck else would he smile at the camera like that and tell the guy recording to get a close up shot?

I felt bad for Isaac. I really did. But not bad enough to not want to watch the video again.

Just as I began to unfasten my jeans so I could watch Isaac's downfall for a second time, three knocks echoed from the front door. Three ill-timed knocks that totally ruined what was to be a very unethical wank.

Chapter 6

DAMIAN WAS WATCHING the television, leaning back on the couch next to me. His legs, clad in grubby black track pants, were spread wide and encroaching into my territory. It was his unexpected visit, asking if he could have a shower, that had robbed me of an unethical wank. That was an hour ago and he still hadn't had the shower he'd asked for, but he had helped himself to two of Gavin's beers, made himself a sandwich and was now relaxing here in the lounge as he made use of our Netflix account.

While Damian giggle-snorted his way through an episode of the inbetweeners, I let my mind wander back to the video of Isaac. More specifically, I wondered whether or not I could handle a similar video of myself find its way onto the website. On one hand it seemed preferable to a tattoo. Sex videos, if done right, could be flattering and had been known to launch careers. But then I wasn't a d-list celebrity or fame-hungry heiress.

So maybe the tattoo was the more sensible option...

But do you really want Jockey's name permanently etched into your skin?

I inwardly shuddered at the disturbing visual of Jockey's name tattooed across my chest.

"This show is such a fucking crack up," Damian said, as he finished off his beer.

He placed the empty can between his legs on the couch, and I naturally turned my head while glancing down. I missed the can altogether and instead found myself noticing his crotch—something I realised I'd done several times since he had arrived. I hastily turned away and stared back at the television.

Why the hell do you keep looking at it?

The answer was both simple and complex.

The simple part was that I was horny. Trapped arousal was still circling inside my balls ever since Damian had unknowingly interrupted what was to be my second wank of the day.

The more complex reason was that I could not stop thinking about the rough fuck the meth-head had dished out on Isaac's asshole. Although my dick was nowhere near the size of the dude in the video I was desperate to see if I could make a man moan with the power of my cock. I had never done that. Never fucked another man. Or woman for that matter. The only part of my virginity I had lost was in the backdoor, and knowing I was only days away from losing the ability to penetrate anyone for the foreseeable future, I found myself viewing Damian—someone I knew who would bite the pillow for cash—as a very real possibility.

Beneath his drug-fucked exterior of bad skin and shabby clothes there was a resonance of innocence; something, somewhere in the mahogany eyes that I found captivating. I had never really viewed Damian Takarangi in a sexual light before. He'd always struck me as a typically average guy with typically average looks—brown eyes, slightly flat nose, full lips, black, wavy hair and that infectious giggle-laugh most Māori boys I knew shared. The one thing about Damian that had been above average had been his bulging muscles, and he'd been popular with the ladies in his younger days because of them, but thanks to the drugs those once mighty muscles of his had withered away and his physique now also resided in average territory.

Yet despite his looks residing in the heart of average central, I had to admit there was still something very fuckable about him in this moment. Maybe it was those long legs of his spread out in masculine nonchalance, or that promising bulge that alluded to something above average. It might have even been the fact he was sitting right beside me while ignoring my existence. These things all combined to give off a distinctly male energy, one dripping with unearned arrogance. I found it both rude and intoxicating in equal measure.

Leaning a little closer towards Damian, I could smell the mist of sweat that baked off him, and the stench of dirty laundry. It was a hot day outside, humid and hot, and he still insisted on wearing that leather jacket of his and stewing in his own sweat. He definitely needed the shower he'd come here for.

Damian picked up the empty can from between his legs and leaned over the end of the couch to place it on the floor. When he settled back down to face the television, he widened his legs a little more, this time one of them coming to rest against mine. The warmth of his touch did not help my blue balls and I found myself wishing we were both wearing shorts so we could be skin to skin.

As he gave his balls a good scratch, I couldn't resist sneaking another look at his crotch. My cock hardened as I thought about how for the right price I could reach inside those black trackies and play with his dick to my heart's content. As I continued to stare at the soft black material covering his sweaty crotch, I found myself licking my lips and thinking about his scribbled advert in the Hickford Park toilets and how it promised a big dick.

I peeked up to find his squinty eyes fixed on mine, invading my brain. Flooded with embarrassment, I quickly turned my attention towards the television.

Shit, I've been caught.

Cringing internally, I waited for him to say something.

"Is it okay if pause the show so I can go take a shower?" he asked.

The silence was deafening as he waited for me to respond. I felt sick and my face burned. I expected the worst when I finally turned to face him again, but I immediately calmed down when I realised that what I had thought was perception was actually his usual drug-fucked gaze. "Yeah, man. Go have your shower. We can finish watching the episode when you get back."

"Cheers, bro." His smile broadened and a chill raced through my arm into my stomach. "You're a good guy, Mike Freeman. A real good guy."

Guilt soon mingled with the chill in my gut. If only he knew the sort of thoughts I had been having about him this past hour.

Damian got up at a sloth's pace and went and rifled through the backpack he'd brought with him, fishing out his toothbrush and a clean change of clothes. Watching him leave the room, my gaze burned into the ass of his pants, imagining how good it would feel to bury my cock between his ass cheeks.

Stop thinking about Damian like this, I scolded myself. *It's wrong. So fucking wrong.*

Ignoring my inner voice's perfectly good advice, I imagined myself fucking my former babysitter and living out an array of kinky fantasies: cuffing him to the headboard and dripping candle wax until he begged me to stop; fuck him hard and deep, spanking him, slapping his face and calling him my bitch, tossing him to delirium with my tongue, then fucking him some more, doggy-style, till he cried.

After five more minutes sat there nursing a stubborn boner, my feet impelled me forward as if by gravitational pull towards the bathroom. Every step I took was a challenge, a battle between the devil on one shoulder and the angel on the other. I knew I was about to do something bad, very bad.

The bathroom door was cracked open, steam filtered through. It smelled warm and the steam was scented with Gavin's Irish-named soap. I pushed it open, looked toward the shower door. I could see Damian's blurred outline through the opaque surface, in the mist, the sound of the water beating against his flesh. His fingers pulled the sliding door open. His drenched face grinned through the downpour at me. "Do you need me to get out?" he asked. "Sorry if I'm taking too long."

"It's not that." I looked at the floor as I tried to force my mouth to speak. "The thing is...I might know someone who'd be keen to pay you for your services."

"What services?"

My throat grew tight. "The ones you offer at Hickford Park."

I forced my eyes from the floor and met his gaze. His expression gave nothing away. Judging by his glazed eyes and the thin set of his mouth it was as if I had just read aloud from the dictionary. I wondered if he hadn't heard me, or if he was still deciding whether to jump out naked and beat my ass.

Finally, after what felt like a million little heartbeats, Damian rubbed the stubble on his chin and said dozily, "Oh, right. *Those* services."

"But this friend of mine would need to know how much."

"That depends on what he's after."

"Everything," I said, all too quickly. "Like, how much would it cost for him to have you for a night."

"A whole night?"

"Uh, more like three or four hours."

"So this friend of yours has told you he's looking for multiple rounds of sex with a stranger he'll pay cash to?" His brown eyes turned doubtful, like he could tell I was making this up. "I think you might be telling me porkies, bro."

I'd half-expected this so I spat out the story I'd prepared before walking in. "It's my mate Jayden. He thinks he might be bisexual but he's never been with a guy to really know. He was telling me recently what he'd ideally want is one night with a guy to just explore things to find out what he's into. The problem is he doesn't know anyone he can try it with, and at a pace he'd be comfortable with, but he reckons there's a lot he wants to try."

"Why doesn't he just hook up with you?"

"Umm..."

He laughed, low and quiet, a purr in his chest "I'm just kidding, bro. I can help your mate out. Show him the ropes so to speak."

"What if he wants to do more than just be shown the ropes?"

"What do you mean?"

"Like, what if he wants to try some kink?"

"I can handle a bit of kink. But I draw the line at some dude taking a shit on my chest."

His blunt response left me speechless.

"Do you know if he's into that?" Damian asked, leaning a little further forward until I caught a glimpse of his wet pubes. "Cause if he is then it's a no go."

"He's not into that sort of thing."

"Well, in that case if he wants my company for a few hours then tell him its three-hundred." He sounded so confident in the amount but almost immediately he added, "But if that's too much I could knock fifty dollars off."

Under normal circumstances it would be far too much but I still had my winnings from the scratchie ticket I hadn't spent yet. "He should be able to manage the three hundred," I said.

"Cool bananas. Are you able to give me his number so me and him can arrange a meet?"

I opened my mouth to tell Damian the truth, that I was the mystery Jayden, but nothing came out. I couldn't do it face to face. It would have to be done later via text—the sensible coward's way.

"Do you know if this Jayden fella will be free to meet up on Tuesday?" Damian asked.

"You don't have to wait till Tuesday. He can meet you tonight."

"Nar. I'm too fucking knackered. You reckon he wants me for a few hours, right?"

"Yeah."

"I haven't done many big jobs like that and I need some time to mentally prepare for that sort of thing. Most of my job are wam-bam-thank-you-Māori-man sort of gigs. They don't usually last longer than ten or fifteen minutes. If that."

"How come?"

"Because when you're getting fucked in a public toilet you both wanna get it over with pretty quick. So if this Jayden wants me for three or four hours, and at a bargain fucking rate might I add, then he better make sure his ass can meet me on Tuesday."

"I'm pretty sure he'll be able to meet Tuesday."

"And make sure you tell him to keep his waha shut. I do this shit on the downlow. I don't want people round here finding out what I do to get by, and I sure as shit don't want anybody finding out I let a school boy root me for cash."

Rather than correct him about his client being a school boy, I joked, "I can tell him to wear his uniform if you like."

"If that's what he wants then sure," Damian replied in an even tone, unable to detect the humour in my remark. "The man with the cash is the man in charge."

Something about what he said sent a dark shiver down my spine, and it wasn't entirely unpleasant.

"I won't know him, will I?" Damian asked, suddenly looking concerned. "The last thing I need is to be sat at the tavern sharing a pint with some bloke whose son I hooked up with."

We might have ourselves a problem there...

Rather than come clean, I just shook my head. There were 48 hours to let him know who the client actually was. I just hoped he wouldn't freak out when I did.

Chapter 7

LATER THAT EVENING, Gavin and I were in our usual positions in the lounge: him stretched out on the couch and me fighting for room at the end with his feet. Unlike the past week, my close proximity wasn't fuelled by my neediness to be near him. It was because I wanted a good view of the television so I could watch the latest episode of Love Island.

The show was utter trash, and I'm sure most critics considered it "low brow" entertainment, but like millions of others Gavin and I enjoyed horny, drama-packed television. Unfortunately for Gavin his enjoyment was bringing him actual physical pain. Every few minutes I'd hear him *hiss* in pain, an indication his cock was trying to get hard inside its cage. He hadn't told me that but I knew from the five days wearing the cage that was what I had experienced.

It probably should have bothered me more knowing my stepfather was trying to sprout wood right next to me, but it was actually sort of funny to know how often the man was turned-on in the space of an hour. The timing of his pained hissy growls confirmed what I already knew; Gavin preferred blondes. Each time a bikini-clad blonde appeared on screen he'd make that noise, followed by his hand reaching down to pat his crotch.

When the show finished, he got up to fetch himself a beer while I stayed seated.

"Did you help yourself to a few beers today?" he asked when he returned with a bottle of Corona in his hand. "All good if you did but just make sure you get some more."

"Sorry," I said. "I let Damian have a couple."

"Damian?" Gavin rolled his eyes. "Did you let that critter inside again, did you?"

"He needed a shower."

"You're too nice for your own good. You should tell the prick to go scrub himself clean in the river."

"He's not that bad."

"Oh yes he is. I told you the other night about the stories I've heard."

"Emphasis on *stories*," I said. "Which means they're probably fictional."

"I can tell you one story that isn't fictional." Gavin chuckled to himself. "He came into the tavern the other night, high as a fucking kite, barely able to walk straight, and came over to sit with me and Trent, uninvited might I add, and proceeded to tell us about how he'd decided to give himself the nickname *Big D* on account of the size of his cock."

Judging by the expectant look on Gavin's face I think I was supposed to find that funny, but instead it just got me horny knowing that if all went to plan then I'd know myself if Damian lived up to the nickname.

Gavin looked at me like he was waiting for me to laugh. "Don't you think that's a bit fucking embarrassing?"

"Maybe he does have a big dick."

"That don't make it any less fucking cringy." Gavin took a swallow of his beer. "You don't go telling people what your dick's nickname is."

"Well, no, but that's because most guys don't give their dicks a name."

"Don't they?"

"Don't tell me you have a name for your dick?" I leered theatrically at his crotch.

He winked, saluting me with the beer bottle.

Smirking, I said, "On second thought, you're right. It is fucking cringe."

"Oi, don't be lumping me in with that jobless dipshit. The difference is I ain't going around telling everyone what my fella's name is."

"And what is its name?"

"You've hurt his feelings so he ain't introducing himself now."

I rolled my eyes. "What a shame."

"Honestly though, Damian Takarangi is a scumbag and you'd be wise to keep your distance. He's probably only coming here and asking to use our shower to see what he can fucking pinch."

"We don't have anything worth pinching."

"Nuh-uh." Gavin pointed his beer bottle at the framed All Blacks jersey on the wall. "That baby there is worth several grand."

"As if. It's just a smelly jersey with a signature on it."

"But it's the signature of Colin Meads *on* the jersey he wore when he played his last match. That's Kiwiana memorabilia of the highest order. It should be in the national museum."

Gavin may have had a point about its Kiwiana value, but that didn't always translate to dollars. It wasn't like a centuries-old suit of armour worn by Henry the VIII.

"If you're gonna stay sat there then make yourself useful," Gavin said, swinging his feet on my lap. "Foot rub time."

This was his jokey way to get me to get off the couch but I surprised us both when instead I grabbed one of his feet and started to massage it.

"I was only joking," he said guiltily.

"It's fine," I said, then foolishly added out loud what I was actually thinking. "I probably need the practice."

Gavin's eyebrows shot up. "The practice, aye? Is this for the sexy vampire?"

Blushing, I pressed my thumbs into the arch of his foot. "That's the one."

My contract with Jockey stated that I'd need to be on hand most days when he returned home from work so I could rub his feet for him. I wasn't looking forward to that, especially knowing how rancid Jockey's feet would probably be after a hard day's work labouring.

Gavin began chuckling. "In that case, I suggest you get as much practise as you can because I love getting my feet rubbed."

I'd never given anyone a foot rub before but I can't have been doing too badly because Gavin looked like he was positively melting into the couch. Especially when I worked on his toes.

Maybe it won't be so bad doing this for Jockey each day, I thought. *My little daily chore to make my man feel good.*

It probably helped it was Gavin's feet I was rubbing because of how used to them I was. He'd used my lap as a makeshift footrest for years during our nights in watching television. Unintentionally, I found myself comparing my stepfather's size twelves to Jockey's skinny feet. Gavin's feet were larger, more manly-looking and obviously less pale, with endearing little hirsute tufts on the tops of each foot. Most importantly they had no foul odour to speak of.

"Tickle my toes," he said, sounding like he was ordering something at a drive-through window.

My fingers granted the order he placed, tickling the underside of his surprisingly attractive toes. He sighed happily, melting deeper into the couch. It felt good to gift him a little pleasure, even if it were just so I could hone my slavish craft.

"Have you ever—" Gavin said, his voice husky. He took a breath and didn't finish his sentence. He looked thoughtful, and for a long time didn't say another word. Then: "Are you thinking about the sexy vampire right now?"

It took me a second to process the question. "No. Why?"

"Because...." His heel pressed down on my crotch, digging into the hard mound of my *erect* cock.

I pushed his feet away, like they'd given me an electric shock; the real shock being that I hadn't even realised I had a boner.

He laughed. "Fiona said my feet were sexy but I didn't realise how sexy."

"It's not because of your feet, dick," I snapped, pressing down on my crotch. "It's from Love Island."

"I don't care what it's from, just keep rubbing them." He dangled his feet above my lap. "Pwetty pwease? You were doing such a good job, Mikey wikey."

Ugh. He was disgustingly adorable sometimes.

Swayed by his cutesy voice, I grabbed hold of his feet and was about to resume the massage when he said, "Just try not to get too excited this time. I don't fancy leaving the couch just to wash your ball juice off my foot."

I gave his feet a hard slap, twice, then stormed over to sulk in the armchair.

Gavin's feet quickly claimed the empty space, and he began to laugh his ass off. "I love family time with, Mikey. Always good for a laugh."

"Laugh at this, bitch," I said, flipping him the finger.

And that's what he did, laughed some more, until eventually I too saw the funny side and joined in.

Chapter 8

MONDAY CLOSING SHIFTS at Chaos dragged more than any other night of the week. This was hardly surprising considering Moa Hill was far from being what you'd consider a booming metropolis with 24/7 nightlife. If it weren't for the café side of the business—which I assumed turned a healthy profit during the daytime—then Chaos would have gone down the gurgler long ago. Despite the bar side of things being nothing but a money-sucker, Carol the owner remained determined to maintain a nighttime presence, insisting Moa Hill needed a "classy weeknight hangout for the town's professional class."

The gossip amongst the staff was that the real reason for the business adding nighttime drinking establishment to its offerings was for Chad's benefit. Carol's son was not the business savvy go-getter like his wealthy parents were and at twenty-five was still relying on them to fund his party lifestyle. At first this had really annoyed me but like a fungal infection the pussy-mad hipster had grown on me. Yes, he was a dick, and yes, his stories of discovering himself on worldwide travels bored the shit out of me, but I had grown to quite like the big oaf and enjoyed working with him—mostly because he let me chill out back under the guise of cleaning while he manned the bar. This allowed my introverted ass to avoid customers while his extroverted ass flirted with anything with a pair of tits that stepped foot inside the bar.

Tonight was proving no exception with Chad out the front hitting up two girls sat at the bar. Meanwhile I was pretending to be busy cleaning down the kitchen in between sending and receiving texts from Damian.

My former babysitter was under the impression the person texting him was Jayden—the fictitious client interested in hiring his services. I had intended to tell him it was me but the more we text the more I kept putting off coming clean. Obviously I'd have to tell him the truth eventually but I was happy for now to let it slide and promised myself that tomorrow I would let him know.

The first thing we had discussed via text was just how much a night of his company would cost me. He'd been cagey at first, pissing me off by not specifying an amount, but eventually he did quote Jayden the same $300 he'd told me the day before. On one hand I knew this was way more than what Damian would ordinarily charge at Hickford Park but I also knew from a quick google search this was a fucking bargain rate for four hours. It was also a bargain because of how much Damian was willing to do—which I'd found out asking my former babysitter a long list of personal questions:

How big is your cock?

Are you circumcised?

Do you swallow?

Can I tie you to the bed?

Can I spank you?

Can I call you a bitch while I fuck you?

His answers weren't as detailed as I would have liked but they revealed that Damian Takarangi would be very accommodating to my wishes.

Pretty big.

Uncut.

Yea bro. I'll eat ur cum.

Yes.

Yes.

U can call me watever u like bro.

Curious to see just how far he was prepared to go, I sent a text asking him if I could piss in his mouth. It wasn't something I'd ever considered doing with a guy but...*maybe?* Before he could respond, I turned the question into a demand:

I plan on using your mouth as my toilet so you better be cool with drinking my piss.

Several times three dots appeared as Damian typed, and stopped, and typed again. I wondered what he wanted to say. Up until now he had been firing back messages at a rapid-fire speed. But now there was a lag...and eventually the three dots disappeared altogether and did not return. I began to worry that I had scared him off. Could I blame him though? I had just told the guy his mouth would be my toilet. He must have thought this Jayden kid was a total freak!

Relief swept through me ten minutes later when I finally received another message. My relief was short-lived though when I saw the message was from Gavin asking if I could buy some groceries on the way home.

Mike: Sure. What do you need?

Gavin: Milk. Bread. Mandarins. Toilet paper. Sizzlers. Margarine. And then stop off and pick us up some Indian for dinner. I'll put the money over to your account.

Mike: Is that all you need?

It wasn't all. For the next hour my phone went off every few minutes with Gavin adding another item to the grocery list. After what felt like the hundredth message, I told him to have a think about everything he wanted then send it all in one message before I finished work.

Gavin: Good thinking batman.

I rolled my eyes. How had he not thought of such a practical approach to begin with?

With Gavin busy compiling a proper grocery list, my phone went quiet. I decided to flick Damian another message: a long row of question marks: *??????????*

He still didn't respond.

Perhaps it was for the best. Paying Damian for sex probably wasn't a good idea. Actually, there was no probably about it. It was a terrible idea. Who in their right mind fucks the man who used to babysit them?

Me apparently if given the chance.

Which is why I'd be lying if I said I wasn't disappointed about scaring him off. In the space of 24 four hours I had managed to convince myself Damian Takarangi was hotter than I'd ever given him credit. Provided he was freshly showered, and bent over the end of my bed, then I would have really enjoyed fucking the guy. There would have been a perverse thrill in knowing the next time I saw him my cock had been inside him. I wondered if that's how Jockey felt these days when he looked at me? A hole that was claimed. A walking sign of his virility?

Shelving my introspection, I returned to cleaning the kitchen and did my best to forget the whole Damian thing. I'd spent too long fantasising and trying to psychoanalyze my desires. It was time for me to focus on the moment and not what-ifs.

AN HOUR LATER, STILL pretending to be busy cleaning, my daydreaming was interrupted by Chad coming into the kitchen to inform me he was going for his last break. I suppressed the groan at knowing this meant I'd have to go man the bar.

"No worries," I said, despite worrying just how long this break of his would be. Some nights Chad had a bad habit of turning fifteen minutes into an hour.

"You should be alright on your own. We've only got one punter out there."

"Coolies."

The tall hipster walked towards me and lifted his hand for a high-five as he walked past to go to the break room AKA the alley behind the café where he would no doubt smoke a joint and spend God-only-knows-how-long talking shit with any drifter passing by.

I put down the cloth I'd been pretending to wipe the benches down with and made my way out front to keep an eye on our lone customer. My feet came to a jolting halt though when I saw who the customer was.

Slumped on the barstool, Jockey's sinewy body oozed provocative arrogance the way his dusty work boots hooked aggressively on the middle rungs, knees propped up and legs spread open. My gaze of course went to the ensnaring sight of his bulge, the thick swell of threadbare material framed by his spread legs. When I finally glanced up, I found him smiling at me.

I went and stood behind the bar where he was sat. "So what brings you here?" I asked.

"You, silly. I came to see how my faggot is."

I coughed up a smile, unsure how I felt about being addressed as his faggot in my place of work. His eyes zeroed in as I slipped my hand under my shirt and scratched lazily at the fuzz around my navel

"And how is your little cock?" he asked.

I blinked, thrown for a second, then said, "It's fine."

Placing his bottle down on the bar with a loud *thunk*, he blurted, "Can you guess what I jerked off thinking about this morning?"

The loud question was random as fuck and totally something Jockey would say, but my response was swift and sharp: "Your aunt's crusty old tits?"

That made him smile. "Funny guy."

"I like to think so."

"I jerked off thinking about you shoving that water pistol in your ass. The one you filled with Gavin's come." He waggled his eyebrows. "That's given me as many boners as it has laughs since I read that."

I knew he was just trying to get a rise out of me so I humoured him with a light chuckle. "I'm glad to see you're finding my moments of shame such good entertainment."

"Ain't nothing shameful about it. I just said I think it's hot."

"I think we might have different ideas of what constitutes shameful."

"I was thinking," Jockey said, watching the liquor swirl in his bottle as he picked it up again, "that I might make you do it again so I can watch. But this time we'll make sure it's filled with my cum, not Gavin's."

I cringed inwardly, outwardly, and every way which one could cringe.

Oblivious to my prudish reaction, Jockey slid off the bar stool and stood up straight, and pulled his jersey up and over his head. For a brief moment, his white t-shirt underneath was dragged up with it, and a long stretch of summer-kissed torso was exposed. I experienced a full-body clench at the sight of his abs and the dark hair that trailed from his navel down into his pants. His work pants hung low enough for me to see the tips of his pubes, the enticing suggestion of bigger, sexier things further south...

When he tugged the hem of his t-shirt back down, he broke my trance and I looked up to take in the rest of him, arms now bare below the short sleeves of his t-shirt. He scratched the stubble on his neck, oblivious to the way my eyes moved over his forearm and down to his wrist and right hand—the hand that had played with himself while thinking about me shoving a water pistol up my ass.

Draping his jumper over the back of the stool, he sat back down and proceeded to inform me about his morning wank. He spared no detail, excitedly telling me how he'd edged himself close to orgasm again and again, how his balls had got so hard they hurt to touch, until eventually he'd nutted and splattered himself with cum up to his chin and open mouth.

While his masturbatory tale had turned me on, especially the part where h admitted to swallowing the cum that had landed in his mouth, I was still glad when we moved on to more SFW topics; like him telling me about his day at work. But that didn't last long, and before I knew it, he'd somehow managed to bring the conversation back to fifteen-year-old me shooting Gavin's cum up my ass with a water pistol.

"What other pervy shit did you do back then?" Jockey asked.

"Nothing."

"Bullshit. I bet you used to sneak into his room and steal his undies to jerk off with."

"Eww. Why would I do that?"

"Cause that's the sort of shit boys do when they fancy someone."

"I never fancied Gavin."

Jockey stared at me as if I'd said something stupid. "There's a reason you put *his* cum into that water pistol, and it wasn't cause your balls weren't producing enough ammo at fifteen. You certainly wouldn't have put the sperm of some crusty old dude in that toy gun knowing where you planned on pulling the trigger."

I winced slightly, saying "Can we talk about something else?"

"I'm not trying to be a dick, I'm genuinely curious. Shit like this fascinates me. You can tell me." He saw my doubtful gaze and then added, "You're talking to the guy who admitted to you he used to suck his brother's dick after school each day. I'm the last fucker who can judge you if you got freaky with Gavin's smelly gruts."

"I never jerked off with Gavin's gruts..." There was an implied *but* hanging in the air that did not go unnoticed.

"But?"

"*But* there may have been a brief moment in time, and I do mean very brief, where I sort of, uh, maybe...liked him a little?" Somehow it came out sounding more like a question than a confession.

"You jerked off thinking about him, you mean?"

"A couple times."

To my relief, Jockey didn't laugh or mock. He just nodded, looking intrigued. "What did you like about him?"

"I dunno. Just that he was nice, I guess."

"Pfft. A guy doesn't tug one out over a personality. You were tugging one out thinking about his cock or asshole. One or the other."

"It was his chest if you must know. And his armpits."

"His armpits?" A horny smile breached Jockey's lips. "Did you wanna lick them?"

I went to say no but the truth tumbled out instead. "Yeah. Fuck knows why. It's not exactly a body part I'm into but I always liked the look of Gavin's for some reason." Jockey's lack of a smirk or piss-taking grin made me feel safe to share a little more with him. "This might sound strange but Gavin always smells nice. Even without deodorant. I guess I thought that if I licked under his arms I could taste the smell I liked so much."

"Does his smell still turn you on?"

"No," I said firmly. "I'm not even sure if his smell turned me on back then. It was more the fact that when I smell him I think of home... Gavin's home."

I suddenly felt like I'd overshared, exposed the true level of my neediness, and I worried what Jockey might say.

I needn't have worried.

"And his dick, right?" Jockey stared at me blankly. "You got off thinking about his dick?"

"Yes, Jockey," I replied, trying not to laugh. "I used to think about his dick."

"When did you last rub one out thinking about the old G-star?"

"Years ago. Like I said, it was a very brief phase, and I don't think it was ever a proper crush. More like adoration of a big brother type." When I saw Jockey's playful smirk I quickly added, "A big brother you don't suck off."

"You say that like it's a bad thing."

That made me glare at him, but Jockey didn't look embarrassed in the slightest. His dark eyes twinkled, fucking twinkled in response.

"So what do you like most about me?" he asked, raised an arm and sniffed his pits. "Is it my smell too?"

This was an easy question. "Your ass. Definitely your ass."

"My ass?" Jockey raised one impish eyebrow. "Really?"

"Yep. I reckon you would have the sexiest ass of any guy in town. Which is why it sucks I'll never be allowed near it."

"You're allowed near my ass. Just not with your cock."

"You'll let me finger you?"

"No, fool. You're gonna be rimming me most days once the contract starts. It's the reason I'm planning on buying a beanbag. I'm thinking you could lie down on it and then I can just sit on your face and play video games. A few hours each night of doing that and you'll be an ass-licking pro in no time."

I loved the look of Jockey's ass but I wasn't sure how I felt about licking it. What if it was sweaty? Or smelly? What if he hadn't wiped properly after taking a—

"Before I forget, check these out." He pulled two pieces of paper out of his pocket—one blue, one yellow. "I finally got around to making the consent forms we're gonna use."

"Consent forms?"

"They were mentioned in the contract."

I'm sure they were. A gazillion things were mentioned in the contract. The fact I couldn't recall them told me it was something less degrading. Or at least I hoped so.

"This yellow one here is what I'll give you if there's another alpha I want you to service. It won't happen often, but you never know when I might owe someone a favour and need to loan you out." He handed me the yellow form to have a look at. "You'll see there are boxes for the date and time, and the name of the guy. Then beneath that will be a description of what you'll be expected to perform. It won't be a lot, not to begin with. I'd rather be the one breaking you in."

Now I remembered reading about the consent forms. As Jockey's personal property he had the right to lend me out. That had been one of the more worrying parts of the contract but my fear was alleviated somewhat by the part Jockey had written about how the borrower would not be allow to damage me in any way.

"Now this one," he said, handing me the blue form, "is what you fill out if you wish to meet up with someone. It doesn't matter if it's a social outing or a sexual outing. I expect a consent form. Most of the time I will decline. I don't just let any cunt use my car so why would I let just anyone use my faggot."

"Fair point."

"So if you ever feel the need to get dirty with Gavin's daddy dick then all you got to do is fill out one of the consent forms. I'd probably approve it too. I like Gav. It'd be good for him to know what a good little cocksucker he helped raise."

"Gavin and me are *never* happening."

"Whatever. But just remember the consent forms will be at my place and I expect you to use them."

I studied the blue form in my hand. It asked for the date and amount of time I would be gone. It also asked who and what sort of outing it was.

"There's more on the other side," Jockey said.

I flipped the page over and saw columns asking for the man's details: age, height, body type, cock size, shoe size. Then a big box at the bottom was where I would fill out what happened during the outing.

"I can't decide if you're a control freak or a kinky genius."

"Probably a bit of both." His smile pulled up one corner of his mouth and he looked completely destructive. "Do you like the idea of asking for my permission?"

"In a weird fucked-up totally unhealthy way...I sort of do."

"That's why you and me are so perfect together."

"Who knows...I might end up your boyfriend yet."

Stunned silence slapped me in the face and I realised my joke had not been well-received.

"That's never happening," Jockey said, deadpan. "I fuck you. I don't date you."

"I do know that."

"Do you?" He eyed me, wary. "It's important you don't get the wrong idea here, Mike. You're my faggot. Nothing more, nothing less. I will take care of you but I will never respect you enough to want to date you."

"You make it sound so romantic."

"It is what it is."

I dreaded to ask the question dancing on my tongue but it had to be asked. "How long do you think we will last? As a faggot and alpha."

"Depends if you plan to renew the contract when the year is up."

"Assuming I did? How long then?"

"Hard to say. I enjoy your company so it's not like I'll ever get bored of spending time with you. That's why we were mates before you gave up the goods. But it is inevitable that you'll eventually get too loose for me. So maybe after three or four years I'd be in the market for a new faggot with a less fucked-out pussy. My dick's not as big as you think, just a whisker under seven inches, which means there will come a time you'll need to be passed onto someone bigger who can handle such a loose cunt."

Jockey had just pissed all over me with is own brand of truth juice. It hurt. It humiliated. But it also turned me on. That was the fucked-up part. There was a thrill in knowing he would drag me to the depths of depravity and leave me wrecked and ruined. But he would never be dishonest about it. I respected that. I could work with that.

"Why don't we go sit down in one of the booths so you can let me give you a foot rub."

"As nice as that sounds, I'm kind of at work if you couldn't tell."

"And if you couldn't tell it's kind of fucking dead."

"Well, that's true."

"And after I've given you a foot rub perhaps we can nip into the toilets so you can..." He made a blowjob motion with his fist, moving his tongue in his cheek.

"We'll see," I said with a half-grin.

"Is my bitch is playing hard to get?"

"I guess you'll find out if you leave here tonight with blue balls or not."

Jockey licked his lips, reaching to scratch the back of his neck. "I suggest you make the most of being a cocktease, Mikey, because come Friday you'll be nodding to every order I give you."

I could not tell if that was a threat or him flirting. It could have been both considering his sexual interests.

Like a fish being pulled in on a line, I followed him over to a booth in the far corner of the bar. After swinging my feet onto his lap, Jockey wasted no time freeing me of my shoes. He dropped the first shoe to the floor under the table but the second one he raised to his face, placed the foot hole over his nose, and sniffed.

"What the fuck are you doing?" I squawked.

"Just taking a sniff."

"Don't do that. They'll fucking reek. I've been on my feet all day."

"It doesn't smell that bad." To prove his point he took another whiff, like he was wearing an oxygen mask. "It's actually sorta sexy."

"You're grim, dude."

"Don't be that grossed out. This is the sort of thing you'll be doing to my shoes once your contract starts."

"I fucking hope not."

He laughed and proceeded to peel away my socks before gathering both feet in his hands and lifting them up to his lips. He planted a little soft butterfly kiss on the arch of each foot, and then started in on my toes. It was nothing drastic nor fierce—just the gentlest light licking and figure-eighting—all in and around, each toe delicately laved and caressed with his tongue.

In the back of my mind was the worry of *what if Chad walks in and sees us?* But I pushed the fear aside, telling myself that we'd have plenty of warning by the sound of the heavy-footed hipster approaching through the kitchen.

While I melted into the generous rubs and licks, I found myself grateful for Jockey's foot fetish. These foot rubs he liked to give were sexual in a way I didn't know sexual could be, reminding me that there was more to a body than genitals. It was as if my cock was hardwired to the soft arch of my foot, each time Jockey's thumb or tongue pressed there I could feel my dick harden a little more. He had just stared to lick my heels and ankles, moaning like he was about to demand me for that blowjob, when my phone dinged with a text.

Jockey lowered my spit-soaked feet to his lap. "Who's texting you?" he asked, sounding like a jealous boyfriend.

"It'll be Gavin sending me the grocery list." I fetched my phone from my jeans to answer the text, but it slipped from my fingers and fell on the floor towards Jockey. Still holding my feet, he hunched down and picked the phone up, taking a quick squizz at the screen before handing it back to me with a goofy smile. "Gavin sure has some fucking weird grocery requests."

I wondered what Jockey was on about until I saw the message.

Damian: I'll drink as much of your piss as you like but it will cost you extra. $350 all up."

Silence ticked between us as I reluctantly met Jockey's gaze. I'd never had a good poker face. Jockey could probably read every guilty thought running through my head.

His eyes darkened in understanding, and he looked me over as if inspecting an animal caught in a trap. A gorgeous, deadly smile tugged at his mouth. "So tell me...who's this Damian guy that's planning on drinking your piss?"

I swallowed thickly, closing my fists around sweaty hands, saying only, "I can explain."

"You don't have to explain anything to me. You're a free man until Friday. If you want to pay a guy to drink your juice then you can."

"I'm not paying him just for that."

"I fucking hope not. For that much money I'd be expecting a blowie, anal, my house cleaned and a three-course meal."

An image of Damian dressed in a maid's outfit cooking me dinner filled my mind. It wasn't pretty.

"So what does this Damian whore look like?" The way Jockey said *whore* was filled with contempt, and a dash of cruelty. "Is he a good-looking lad?"

"Um..."

"You don't have to tell me...unless you want to."

I didn't want to.

"But seriously, dog, if you're going to pay a homo hooker that much then make sure you get your money's worth."

"I'm not asking him to clean my house if that's what you're getting at."

He sniggered. "No, I'm talking about making sure you last the distance. It would suck if you hand over that much cash and then blow your load in thirty seconds."

The thought I might be a one-pump chump hadn't occurred to me. *Why the fuck hadn't that occurred to me?* I'd never topped before so there was a high to almost certain chance that I'd come quickly. "What do I do to make sure that doesn't happen?"

"Pray that you can learn how to fuck like a stallion before you meet the bitch." And then he laughed his ass off, letting me know just how absurd that suggestion was.

Chapter 9

"CAN I ASK A QUESTION?"

Gavin swallowed his last mouthful of butter chicken and put down his fork. He took a large gulp of beer and wiped his mouth on a square of handy towel. "Last time I checked it wasn't illegal to ask a question in this house."

"It's sort of embarrassing though." I had already finished eating but was still picking at the plastic containers in the middle of the table. I tore off a piece of roti bread and wiped it round my plate to soak up the last of the sauce.

"The only embarrassing questions in this house are the one you don't ask." He took another sip of beer and eyed me over the rim of the glass.

"I was just wondering what sort of advice you could give me to make a night with a girl more exciting. And maybe last a little...longer." I shifted uncomfortably in the chair and glanced out the window. It was dark outside and the brightness of the room made it impossible to see the ranges in the distance.

"So you're worried about losing your lollies too quickly?" he answered after a long pause. "Is that you're saying?"

I nodded and reached across the table for his beer.

"Hey," he protested weakly. I was the only person Gavin would ever let drink from his glass. Something I'd long considered an honour.

"That's better," I said, sliding the glass back to him.

"Does this hypothetical night you're talking about involve your sexy vampire, otherwise known as Lady Lovebite?" he asked, one eyebrow raised.

I nodded again, knowing it was better to go along with an imaginary girlfriend with sharp teeth than tell him I was planning on paying the local sometimes-homeless man for three hours of what I hoped would be mind-blowing sex.

He smiled and took a sip of his beer. "Well, I could tell you to jerk off just before she arrives but that's not always a safe move, and could see you eating her out for God only knows how long until your dick is ready for the main course." He leaned back in his seat and linked his hands behind his head. "But I know a better option."

"Which is?"

"Aside from the obvious answer of foreplay being your friend, there's a trick I sometimes like to use if I know the girl is expecting a marathon and not a sprint. It's to use some toys into the bedroom. A dildo or vibrator to be more specific. Or if you're fucking desperate, and the girl says it's okay, then you can use a vegetable."

"A vegetable!?"

He raised both eyebrows, as if to say "And what?"

"What sort of vegetable?" I asked.

"Bloody hell, Mikey, use your imagination. Anything cock-shaped." Gavin smirked. "Why do you think your mother used to make carrot salad so much."

"Please tell me that's a joke."

That got him laughing. "But in all seriousness, I reckon every guy should own a dildo. Not just ladies and gay dudes. It's important for a bloke to have a spare sword handy, something to go into battle for him when the one between his legs is growing tired. But never let the girl know you're using it because you're tired. Never do that. Just make out you're using it to be a bit sexy, a bit kinky. If Lady Lovebite is anything like Fiona, and a few other women I've been with, then don't be afraid to suck the dildo first before fucking her with it. Lick the tip, try and deepthroat the fucker, make it look like you're giving a real blowie. That shit drives some girls wild. Trust me, you'll be rewarded nicely."

"How do you know how to make it look like you're giving a real blowjob?" I asked with a smirk. "Have you and Stryder already had date night?"

"No ya cheeky shit, but it's not exactly rocket science, is it? You just put it in your mouth and suck."

"Duly noted."

"But I have kissed a guy before," Gavin said with pride, forgetting he'd told me this story many times through the years. "Back in my Invercargill days Trent and I would make out at parties all the time for a laugh. Full on tongue and everything. It was fucking hilarious. The homophobic assholes would call us faggots and tell us we were disgusting, but the all the girls would gather around and egg us on, and you could always guarantee that by the end of the night Trent and I would both be going home with a girl each while the redneck fuckers were left there alone with their blue balls."

Although I'd heard the story countless times, I never interrupted him. There was something good and pure about the story; a pair of idiotic but well-meaning jocks sticking their finger up at conformity and bigotry. It was all the better because of how they came out the winners with the pretty girls in the face of the judgemental bigots. However, I suspect Gavin and Trent's luck had a lot more to do with how good-looking they'd been back in the day, but I never pointed this out to my stepfather. It was better to let Gavin believe he'd been a badass sexual rebel, even if all he and Trent ever did was pash.

"And Trent's a good kisser. Probably in my top three of all time. Which is why..."

You two made a pact at eighteen that if you were both single at thirty you would go gay for one another...

"So it was a damn good thing I met your mother and he met Donna because otherwise I'd be sharing a bed with the hairy brute. But I think we would have made a cute couple. The only problem would have been..."

Deciding who got to be the man and who was the woman. And I don't mean doing the dishes. Trent always said we'd have to play rock, paper scissors each night to decide who got to slip it in...

While Gavin continued with the story I knew word for word, I thought to myself how lucky I was to have such an accepting stepfather, or whatever he was to me. It seemed crazy to think I'd never come out to him, even when I had just thought my interest in guys was a phase. He wouldn't have cared. Shit, he'd probably put a rainbow bumper sticker on his car and offered to go to the Sydney Mardi Gras with me.

Finally done with his story about marrying Trent, Gavin asked, "Where were we? I got a bit carried away."

"Dildos. You said I should buy one."

"That's right. If you are gonna invest in buying a dildo then I recommend getting one the same size as your own dick or smaller.

You don't want to run the risk of being out performed by the dildo. Unless you and the sexy vampire only have a casual thing going and you don't care what she thinks. In that case go as big as you like. It can be fun to take your time and force her to open up."

My dick began to get hard at hearing that and I knew then and there I would be buying something sizable. After all, it wasn't going in my ass.

"I'd offer to lend you mine but it probably wouldn't be appropriate."

Despite him having told me this was a trick he'd used himself in the past, it still surprised me to hear that somewhere in this house was a dildo. "So you actually own a dildo?"

"Yeah. It's a mould of my own cock. An exact replica."

I deadpanned. "You made a mould of your own dick?"

"I sure did. His name is Gavin the Relentless."

The name was adorably stupid, and typical Gavin.

"I can't believe you made a mould of your own dick." I shook my head in disbelief. "That's so crazy."

"Nothing crazy about it. I was blessed with a handsome prick so why not have more than one of it." He spoke without an ounce of shame. "I can buy you a kitset for your birthday if you like? We could have sword fights around the house like Star Wars."

I burst out laughing at the ridiculous image. "So where is Gavin the Relentless?"

"Do you want to see him?"

"I, uh... should, maybe—"

My word salad was put out of its misery when Gavin said, "I don't mind showing you if you want to see him. But he's actually at Fiona's at the moment. She's been using him to get by on account of me being locked up."

"Riiight."

"The cheeky bitch reckons he does a better job than Gavin the Destroyer."

"Who the fuck is Gavin the Destroyer?"

His eyes grew bright, warming his entire face. "The *original* version."

"Oh..."

"I can't wait for this cunting cage to come off so I can prove to her you can't beat an original."

"So when does the cage come off."

"Thursday."

"That's not far away."

"No. Thank fuck."

"And is Thursday when you'll be..."

"Getting christened up my Hershey highway?"

"I wasn't going to be putting it quite like that but...yeah?"

"Yep. Thursday night is the main event. It should be good. Should be fun."

I didn't know if he was trying to reassure himself or me, so I just nodded. "Whatever you say."

"The way Fiona's been going on about it I'm surprised she hasn't started selling ringside tickets." He chugged back another mouthful of beer then let out a burp. "But if she does start selling tickets then I expect you to buy one. I expect you there cheering me on and giving moral support." He started laughing.

I didn't usually mind Gavin's dirty sense of humour; it had entertained me for years. But on this occasion the thought of watching Gavin get fucked wasn't a laughing matter. It felt wrong, and dirty. I blamed my conversation with Jockey earlier. Why? Because it reminded me that once upon a time, albeit briefly, I had viewed Gavin as more than just a father figure. His pheromones had done things to my adolescent brain, spun my wheels in confusing ways, had me craving to kiss him in places where I had imagined he smelled the best. Although those days of longing to kiss his chest and armpits were well behind me—and they really were—I could not deny that it felt wrong to sexualise Gavin even if it was done in the name of humour.

"What's wrong?" Gavin asked. "That was funny. Why aren't you laughing?"

"You know my sexy vampire?"

"Yeah? What's she got to do with anything?"

I gave it a few beats, then, as gently as I could, I told him, "She is actually a *he*." My lips felt numb as I spoke and I found myself looking over his shoulder rather than meeting his gaze. "I don't know if I'm gay or bisexual but I know I'm into guys, a lot, and I just thought it's time you know."

Gavin didn't say a thing, just sat there quietly.

"I don't want you to make a big thing out of it," I continued, knowing the man was a big softie at heart. "No hugs, emotional speeches, or tears of queer joy if that's what your planning on, just be normal and chill." I finally forced myself to meet his gaze and I saw that his eyes were wet. "I told you no tears."

He sniffled and laughed. "Sorry. My tears of queer joy fall on their accord. I can't help it."

Thankfully only two tears fell, one from each eye, which he softly wiped away with a finger and stuck in his mouth. "I always wondered what queer joy tasted like, and now I know."

"And what does it taste like?"

"Honest. Good. Us."

Damn it! Now I had two tears of my own falling and before I could wipe them away I got the hug I had specifically asked him not to give. Hunched over my seated position, Gavin squeezed me tight as if we were on an episode of Fuller House.

Turning in my seat, I slung an arm around his back and returned the hug. I knew the hug was as much for him as it was for me. When we finally let each other go, Gavin returned to his seat, all teary-eyed emotions dealt with, and he began smirking like an asshole.

"What's so funny?" I demanded.

"Nothing." But he kept smirking. "I just want to make a confession of my own."

"And what's that?"

"I've known for a while you might like boys more than girls. That's why I'm so happy you finally felt comfortable enough to tell me."

I suddenly felt incredibly exposed. "How did you know? And if you say my long hair I'll throw my dirty napkin at you."

With a voice that bridged humour and wisdom perfectly, he said, "Because my spidey senses have always worked best on the people I love."

And more tears fell down both our faces.

Chapter 10

WITH NO WORK TODAY I was able to spend the morning at home working on my latest mystery novel. I had sort of lost my mojo with it these past few days so it was good to sit down and get stuck into it again. Although I managed to write two thousand words before lunchtime, the vast majority of them were shit. The only reassuring about that was I knew every writer's first drafts were crap, and I could always fix things when it came to the editing stage.

If I could finish this book then it would be the third novel I had written, and I was hoping for a case of third time lucky since my previous two books had failed to catch the interest of an agent. Each time I usually just received an email of decline that was clearly a generic template. One time though an agent in the US told me the story had a lot of promise but said she was not looking for fiction set outside America. Bugger boots.

With that in mind, I should have been writing a historic mystery set in some misty New England town, or maybe some dusty wild west ranch, but once again I'd gone for a New Zealand setting, partly because I was a stubborn shit but also because it's what I knew. But despite my current novel once again being set in New Zealand, I could not deny that for some reason the story still felt forced...like it wasn't really me.

Excusing my fears of never achieving my dreams of being published, I was still in a super sunny mood today. The main reason for that was because of what I was about to go into town to buy—a dildo for my night with Damian!

It amazed me how a man I had never viewed in a sexual light had been the driving force for 80% of my boners the past forty-eight hours. The more I pictured him naked,bent over and waiting for my cock, the more I realised just how much I was going to enjoy conquering Damian Takarangi's asshole. I still hadn't broken the news to him that I was Jayden, the horny teen with a depraved interest in using his mouth as a toilet, but I figured I'd cross that bridge tonight when we met in person. While that ran the risk of being face-to-face with a thuggish meltdown, I also knew it ran the least risk of him backing out on the deal.

The other reason I was so upbeat was how well things with Gavin had remained after coming out to him. This morning at breakfast he had behaved like nothing had changed between us. The only thing that may have been a bit odd was I could tell he wanted to ask me questions about who the guy was I had coming over tonight. I based that on how he made a point to say "I guess we need to change Lady Lovebite's name to Sir Lovebite."

While I may have had no problem with Gavin knowing I was into men, I wasn't quite so unashamed of who Sir Lovebite actually was—Jockey—or who tonight's guest would be for that matter. Both names would have Gavin pissing his pants in laughter, although I suspected he may have thought the idea of me and Jockey being together was cute and he'd probably want to encourage a spark that didn't exist. But yeah, otherwise shit was honky dory. Gavin had promised to go straight to Fiona's after work so I could have the house to myself, even going out of his way to tell me where to find extra condoms in his room if I needed any.

After working on my novel until my brain was drained of all creative energy, I decided it was time to make the long trek into town so I could buy the dildo.

Just as I was about to leave the house, my phoned vibrated in my pocket. It was a text from Damian.

Damian: Hey Jayden. I've changed my mind. I'll only do 2nite if u pay me 500.

My heart squeezed, and my excitement dug itself a grave to lie down and die in. I felt like I'd just been turned down a dance at a school disco. Disappointment was swifty replaced with anger at my former babysitter's lastminute change of rate. I may have been boiling with rage but my thumb kept its cool as it tapped out a quick reply.

Mike: But we already agreed to 350.

Damian: And now its 500. Wat u want is worth more than 350.

I found that highly debatable considering the low amount he probably charged total strangers at Hickford Park. I shouldn't have been surprised though. A drug-fucked opportunist was always likely to pull this sort of stunt.

Another text came from Damian that pissed me off even more.

Damian: And make sure you've got some booze there for me to drink.

Motherfucker! I was beginning to view Damian in the same negative light as most of my neighbourhood did, although for very different reasons. How fucking dare he suddenly make demands and change the rate. It bugged me how he was trying to wrestle control of what was supposed to be my night.

Damian: Give me an answer in 10 minutes or I will make other plans.

That was the cherry on the shit cake.

I had enough money to give Damian what he wanted, but I wasn't inclined to do that. Sighing, I dragged myself to the lounge where I threw myself on the couch. I spent the next few minutes checking my email, scrolling through my Facebook feed, and catching up on some news. It failed to distract me from what felt like the biggest let-down of the century.

"Gaaah." I tossed the stupid phone on the coffee table but grabbed it immediately again and downloaded the Grindr app. I'd used the app a few times before, mostly just to be nosy. And while talking dirty to random guys was fun, I could never bring myself to follow through on the multitude of invitations for *right-now* hookups. I'd just get off on the dirty chat, jerk off, and delete the virtual meat market just as quickly as I'd downloaded it.

Today's different! If Damian won't meet me then I'll find someone who will. And for free!

I was met by a grid of faces and bodies and I browsed through them. A twink, a hairy daddy, a guy in a cowboy hat—*in New Zealand? Really?*—and a couple headless torsos were on display. A cute Asian guy was a few blocks away or so, and I clicked his picture to find out more about him, but all he'd entered in his bio was an eggplant emoji.

"You gotta be kidding me," I muttered and scrolled ahead.

It didn't take me long to go through them all, and I deleted the app like I always did.

I might have found one or two of them fuckable any other day. But not today. These men didn't carry the level of danger as fucking my former babysitter did. Didn't have that same moral wrong, which I had slowly been discovering was a large part of why the thought of hooking up with Damian turned me on so much.

Bang on ten minutes later, Damian sent another text.

Damian: Deal or no deal? I havnt got all farking day. I need an answer.

"Fuck off you illiterate prick." Rather than text a response I put my phone back in my pocket.

Why did sex have to be such a fucking battle? Jockey had demands. Damian had demands. *Fuck demands and fuck both of them!* I was over it. I'd rather jerk off to porn and cum in a sock for the rest of my life than keep being made feel like I was the one having to meet expectations. My anger with Jockey quickly receded, though, when I acknowledged he was at least open and honest about what he wanted, and he didn't change the rules without warning.

My foul mood with Damian brewed over the next hour, and eventually it was Brian who became the recipient of my hate bubbles as I thought about how he still hadn't contacted me. Asshole. At least Jockey and Damian had excuses. One was thinking with his cock and the other with his wallet. But what was golden boy's excuse? What expectations had I failed to meet of his?

Fuelled by my rage, I finally snapped and messaged him.

Mike: You've been gone for three weeks and I still haven't heard jack from you. What the fuck is your problem?

I immediately regretted sending the text.

There was no way to prevent WhatsApp from hurtling the words to Brian's account, and the message below it stated he had read it less than ten seconds later.

My phone started ringing.

Guilt forced me to close my eyes and I swiped my phone as if reading brail and accepted the call.

"What the fuck is going on?" He was so angry he didn't sound like himself. "Are you going to answer me?"

I opened my eyes. He didn't sound like himself because it wasn't Brian.

It was Damian.

"I told you I needed an answer in ten minutes," my former babysitter growled. "That was nearly an hour ago."

Stunned, panicky, unsure what to do, I stupidly attempted to change my voice into some sort of deep, drawly Kiwi farmer accent. "I been busy, mate."

"Fuck your busy. What's the verdict? Deal or no deal?"

"No deal." I braced myself for an onslaught of abuse.

The silence on his end lasted so long that I glanced at the screen of my phone to see if he'd hung up. He hadn't and when he spoke again, his voice was low and tinged with disappointment.

"I knew you would back out."

"This isn't a case of me backing out, mate, it's me refusing to put up with someone pulling a swifty at the last minute.

"It's not a swifty," he said. "And it's not the last minute. There's still seven hours until we have to meet."

"I still ain't coughing up five hundred bucks. Getting that sort of money outta me is like pulling tits on a bull, mate." I knew I was laying the 'mate' shit on a bit thick but I was committing to this cow cocky accent gumboots and all.

Silence floated down the line once again.

"Fine," Damian eventually said. "We can still meet for the original amount."

"Too late. I've gone and spent it."

"What?"

"I spent the dough, mate."

"What the fuck? It's only been an hour."

"I decided I'd spend it on dog tucker instead." I cringed at my choice in words and sudden change in fake accent; I'd just gone from sounding like a Kiwi hick to a redneck in the Australian outback. Damian didn't appear to notice.

"Fuck the dog tucker. What am I supposed to do? I was relying on that money."

"Then you shouldn't have been a greedy bugger...mate."

"I'm not your fucking mate, bro." Damian sounded like he wanted to scream at me, but he quickly sweetened his tone and said, "Look, how much do you have?"

"Fifty bucks."

"Fifty?" Damian made a pained whining sound. "Is that all?"

"Yep. So if you still keen to do everything we agreed on, but for fifty bucks, then let me know. Bye, mate."

"But—"

I hung up on him, feeling rather pleased with myself—and mightily impressed with my voice acting.

Within seconds my phone lit up with a text.

Damian: U cnt expect a 4 hour session and 2 piss in my mouth for just $50!!!

Mike: That's the offer. Take it or leave it.

I watched the little dots flash across the bottom of our chat window, indicating Damian was responding with a long message. I knew it would be abusive but I didn't care. If I was going to miss out on a night of sex then it was only fair that Damian got to spend the rest of his day in a foul mood.

Damian: OK. I'll do it for 50. Just tell me when and where.

I suddenly realised why these men enjoyed a battle: Because it was fun to feel like you were winning. I was enjoying my victory so much that I even managed to forgot all about the message I had sent Brian.

Chapter 11

TO SAY I WAS FEELING self-conscious as I entered Naughty Nik Naks, Moa Hill's largest adult entertainment store, was an understatement. Not helping matters was the way the dude behind the counter kept looking at me strangely. Tall and thin, and in his mid-to-late thirties, he wore a bright orange beanie that clashed terribly with his ripped, tight black jeans and denim jacket. I couldn't decide if he was keeping an eye on me to make sure I didn't steal a sex toy or if he wanted to use one on me.

The interior of the shop looked pretty much as I had expected it to look. Down the left-hand wall were two displays; one of erotic greetings cards and another of CD's and second-hand records. There was a book stand in the corner, a mix of straight and gay titles, mostly erotica, and next to that, a massive display of porn magazines. Against the wall, directly opposite the door, was a clothing section. On one tiny bit of wall, hung full rubber body suits, naughty lingerie, a nurse's outfit, jockstraps, underwear, as well as whips and harnesses.

Further round from the rubber section was the counter where beanie dude was *pretending* to read a magazine. Over his shoulder, I could see an array of cock rings and leather straps, a variety of masks and bottles of something called amyl nitrate. To the left of the counter was a video unit.

And finally, to the right of the door, was a huge cabinet of sex toys.

There were no other customers.

Too nervous to start browsing the various dildos straight away, I made my way to the magazine rack first and spent ten minutes browsing an array of imported skin-mags. I glanced casually over my shoulder. From behind the counter, beanie dude was still watching. He smiled. I nodded.

As he smiled, his eyes creased with strong laughter lines. There was something familiar about his face. I chalked it down to him looking like most white trash criminals on reality crime shows. The sort of redneck caught drink driving with his four kids in the backseat.

"Is there anything I can help you with?" he asked.

I shook my head. "Not just yet. I'm browsing."

"Okay then. Have a good look round. Let me know if you see something you like."

"Thanks, I will."

I put the magazine back on the shelf. It was time to get what I really came in for. I turned and strode over to the toy section. Now that I was presented with the vast array of fake dicks, I felt completely lost and confused. I almost wished I'd called Jockey and asked him to come with me. At least he knew about this sort of kinky shit.

Christ, I didn't know what to buy. I had never seen such a vast selection of rubber cocks. Spread across five shelves, the dildo display seemed to comprise of every size, shape and colour of toy imaginable. The collection began on the top shelf with a huge three foot long, double ended monster, and went all the way to the bottom with a selection of small, finger-sized plugs. There was every possible combination in-between.

I stared in awe.

Now that I was faced with so much variety, I didn't know what I wanted. Certainly not one of the top shelf beasts that must have been plated in gold to warrant such extortionate prices. I also knew the little finger plugs would be a complete waste of time and money; I could shove my finger up Damian's ass if that's the size I wanted to ram in him.

While I mulled over which dildo was best for the job, I spotted a row of handcuffs on the bottom shelf. They hadn't been on my wish list upon entering the store but seeing the glint of silver had my cock nodding in my pants, imagining the sight of a naked Damian restrained to my bed while I ploughed his ass. I gave in to temptation and decided to buy two pairs of heart-shaped love cuffs for Damian's hands and feet.

Returning my attention to the dildo section, I picked up one that doubled as a vibrator. It was packaged in a black box with a plastic window. The blurb on the side of the pack said it was 8 inches long; *a full 8" of vibrating pleasure to make you squirm and beg for more.* It was moulded in flesh coloured plastic and designed to look like the real thing, with a big crescent head and a string of veins running all down the shaft.

I wasn't sure. It wasn't the length that made me cautious so much as the girth. This thing was huge, like my wrist. Something told me Damian's asshole would struggle with this.

But that's the point, a little voice needled.

And on that sadistic note, I took it to the counter with the love cuffs where I also asked for a bottle of lube and a pack of condoms.

While Beanie rang up my purchases, I couldn't help but look at the tight black jeans he wore. The dark material was wrapped so tightly around his tooth-pick legs it was as if he'd been squeezed inside of them. Especially around the crotch. It was damn near pornographic how blatant his bulge was.

It suddenly seemed a shame to dip into the cash fattening my wallet, so rather than pay with my scratchie ticket winnings, I used my eftpos card, wiping out what was left of my wages from work. When the payment was accepted, Beanie dude slid my items into a brown paper bag.

"Here you go, buddy," he said. "I hope these bring the pleasure you're after."

"They're not for me." I felt myself blushing. "They're for a friend."

Eyeballing me like I was dinner, he dropped his hand to his ample bulge and gave it a slow, deliberate squeeze. Then he reached for a pen and wrote something on the brown paper bag with my goodies in it. "Here's my number. Make sure you give me a call if you encounter any problems with the products. We here at Naughty Nik Naks always aim to please."

I nodded, knowing this was just a blatant come on. "Will do," I said, having no intention to ever call this man whose breath could benefit from a mint.

I was about to step away from the counter when he said, "Or just give me a call if you want something bigger than what's in the box." With a bony hand, he reached up and pulled the orange beanie off to reveal the shaved head underneath. "Moose will help get ya loose."

Chapter 12

FIVE HOURS LATER, MY chance encounter with Moose still had me feeling uneasy. I'd left the store feeling like a baby seal that had just swum through an oil spill; dirty and at risk. Goodness only knows why. It wasn't like he'd accosted me with a weapon and threatened my life—although that over-sized sausage otherwise known as his cock could be considered a weapon of sorts—but he had oozed dark vibes and nefarious intentions. Even if he wasn't a skinhead, which he may well not have been, and if I had never seen the video of him fucking Isaac, I still wouldn't have liked the look of the geezer.

The dude must have had big balls in more than one sense to remain living in Moa Hill considering his face was on the Hickford Homos website for all to see. Mind you, he didn't look like the sort of guy who'd give a rat's ass about his reputation suffering any damage. Fucker would probably revel in it. But that only made him seem more suspect, especially when I thought about how he'd looked right at the camera during his fuck session with Isaac.

Was he the dude behind it all? The one the papers had labelled the homophobic vigilante? That didn't make much sense though. Actually, it made no sense.

Rather than let myself fuss about a guy I had no intention of ever calling, I had spent the afternoon and early evening focusing instead on my date with Damian.

Yes, I was calling it a date, even if it was one I was paying for.

Damian had agreed to meet 'Jayden' outside an abandoned row of shops just a few blocks from my house. The abandoned strip was eerie at night but I wanted us to meet in neutral ground, and somewhere if he had a meltdown not too many people would witness my embarrassment. On the flipside, if he did choose to have a violent meltdown then I only had to run a couple hundred metres to the nearest house. But I was pretty sure that was an unlikely scenario. I figured the guy might be pissed to find out he'd been duped but not fist-happy.

Well...

In an overly cautious approach to my first time paying for sex I had sat down at my laptop earlier and typed Damian's name into google to see if I could find any evidence to support Gavin's claims about Damian being a violent thug. Before the search results had come back I was leaning more towards Gavin being fed bullshit information by the resident gossips at the local tavern.

But then the search results had shattered that notion.

A whispered "Fuck me" was all I'd manage to say when not just one but *five* articles came back that featured Damian Takarangi appearing in court for violent assault charges. It was shocking to find out someone I had considered a nice guy wo was just down on his luck was in actual fact a violent thug with anger management problems. When I read details about how he'd beaten an ex-girlfriend's new lover so badly they needed surgery to save the guy from losing an eye, I very nearly text Damian to tell him the deal was off.

But my horniness won out. Of course it did.

With an hour to go before we were scheduled to meet, I showered, shaved, fussed over my hair, deliberated over my choice of underwear—eventually settling on my grey and pink boxer briefs, which I decided flattered my package the most—changed my outfit after I got dressed because the first one was wrong, checked myself in the mirror way too many times in case I missed a spot shaving or whatever, and flew out the door like I was late to catch a flight.

I just hoped this flight wouldn't crash and burn.

AS I STOOD OUTSIDE the abandoned shops, waiting for Damian to show, I wondered what the game plan would be when we got back to my place. There were so many things I wanted to try but I wasn't sure which order to do them in. All I could be sure of was that by the end of the night I intended to have fulfilled several fantasies.

Gavin had agreed to spend the night at Fiona's and wouldn't be back until the morning. This meant Damian and I would have all the privacy we need. The deal was that Jayden had Damian's sexual services from eight P.M. till midnight. Four hours of sexual debauchery in exchange for fifty dollars. Each time I found myself feeling guilty about paying him so little, I reminded myself it was

Damian's punishment for trying to wrangle more out of the fictitious Jayden than he'd originally agreed to.

When it got to twenty minutes past eight, I began to worry he might not show. Maybe he had come to his senses and realised selling his ass out for less than minimum wage wasn't worth it. While understandable I was still disappointed knowing I had invested in a dildo, love cuffs and a dozen beer for no reason. Add in the condoms and lube, and tonight had cost me nearly two hundred dollars.

Just as I was about to head home for a pity wank, I spotted a dark figure approaching the corner. It was Damian. As he got closer, I was surprised to see he'd put on what appeared to be the cleanest clothes he'd worn in years. His usual mishmash of grubby pants and leather jacket were nowhere in sight. He wore what appeared to be brand new black sweatpants and a baggy black hoody with some rapper on the front—a thuggish but tidy ensemble. Even the white high-top sneakers he wore appeared to have been cleaned. He may have been at the lower end of rent boys but he'd clearly made an effort.

He stood on the street, one hand moving down the front of his pants while I approached him. When he saw me, the confusion on his face confirmed he'd had no idea I was actually Jayden.

"Hey, Mike." He scuffed a shoe on the pavement, looking jittery, like a hyperactive kid on the verge of needing his next dose of Ritalin. "You better not be here to tell me your mate's cancelled."

We stood a few feet away from each other, while Damian's expression went heavy with disappointment. Guilt bubbled inside me. "He hasn't cancelled."

"Then where is he?" Damian's eyes flitted about searching for his client.

"Right here. It's me...I'm Jayden." My voice was far away, like I was eavesdropping on myself.

He turned and stared, looking almost creepy in the dim light, three inches taller than me, peering down from his hood "What the fuck, Mike? Why didn't you tell me you were the client?"

"Because you would have said no."

"Exactly. Which is why you should have told me. We can't do this. I used to be your fucking babysitter for Christ's sake. Shit, I knew you when you were a little fella hanging off your mum's skirt."

"So?"

"So, I don't really wanna pass you in the street and know what you look like naked. Or have you know what I look like naked."

"It's just a body."

"That's easy to say when you're not the one who walks away from tonight knowing you let some kid fuck you for fifty bucks." He shook his head in disgust. "I don't want you looking at me like I'm some cheap hangi pants."

"Half the time you past me in the street you're so fucking high you don't recognise me so what's it matter?"

"It'll matter to me the other half of those times when I do recognise you. I wanna stay the dude who used to babysit you, not some cheap whore you paid for a good time."

I should have felt sympathy for him, and I sort of did, but I also felt arousal. The dark flames of a twisted desire burning the sperm in my balls. I wasn't sure how to play this so I decided to be honest, regardless of how cruel it may come across.

"But that's what I want. To fuck you like the cheap whore you are."

I was numb, disconnected from the world, as if someone had put a snow globe over me. I couldn't believe what I had just said, and neither could Damian judging by the look on his face.

He stepped closer, hands curling into fists "You wanna say that again?"

I almost heard a drum-roll in my head, or the theme to Jaws, but I held firm.

"If you don't want people thinking of you as some cheap whore, Damian, then maybe you shouldn't be a cheap whore. I would have respected you more if you'd held firm and demanded more cash. But you didn't. And now you're here to make a lousy fifty dollars."

"You've got some mighty big balls to speak to me like that, Mike. Mighty big fucking balls."

"The question is do I own *your* big balls for the night?"

"That is the question." His eyes narrowed to nasty slits. "The fifty fuckin' dollar question."

"So do we still have a deal?" I extended my hand until it hovered just a few inches from his crotch.

He zigzagged a glance from my feet to my awaiting hand. After what felt like a small eternity, he jutted his hips forward and pressed his crotch against my open palm. "Have at it, brother. These big Māori balls are all yours for the next four hours."

I groped the warm mound of his bulge, unable to believe I was being given permission to fondle his junk. He trembled slightly, but otherwise remained still, letting me get frisky with his nuts through the material. I couldn't feel any sign of arousal yet, but the night was young.

Chapter 13

THE WALK BACK TO MY place was done under the blanket of an awkward silence. Perhaps that was for the best. I didn't want to risk saying anything that would scare him off before we got to the house. I could feel his nervous energy, clearly still battling between wanting to do what was right—which was telling me the deal was off—and his desperation for my cash.

When we reached the driveway of my home, he made a move toward the house, heading for the front door. I told him "No," and led him to the garage.

I pulled a cord, turning on a naked lightbulb that illuminated dusty concrete floors, rows of shelving, old paint tins, a lawn mower, furniture in storage, and a small refrigerator. In the centre of the garage was an old single bed I had pulled out of the storage area and fitted with clean sheets and a blanket. It wasn't the most romantic of settings but I hadn't felt right hosting a night of debauchery inside the house with a criminal I was paying for sex.

The harsh light bleached the brown skin of Damian's face. He narrowed his eyes against the glare. Now that we were inside I noticed that he'd also gone to the trouble of shaving; Damian with smooth cheeks was a rare event indeed. He took off the rapper hoody and I was pleased to see that underneath he wore a freshly cleaned white t-shirt that contrasted beautifully with the new black pants he had on.

Wasting no time, I latched my hand onto his crotch and began molesting his junk again. The soft flesh beneath his black trackpants remained unresponsive to my touch, but I did not care.

"I can't believe I'm playing with your balls," I mumbled.

"Yeah." His face was unsmiling and unemotional.

With my hand still latched onto his balls, I leaned into him and licked his neck. I felt him shudder. Even if I wasn't the kid he used to babysit then I'm sure this wasn't something he enjoyed doing—to him I probably seemed too young and in any case I was the wrong gender for him—but he was prepared to tolerate what no doubt seemed like a deviant interest for the sake of making some cash.

"Have you got any booze?" he asked, easing away. "My mouth is bone dry."

I told him to take off his shirt while I got him a beer. I watched him as I moved to the fridge. He pulled the t-shirt over his head, revealing a torso that was a shadow of its former glory. He would benefit from a few more meals and a little less drink, I thought, but he wasn't in terrible shape.

I handed him the beer and he wasted no time in wetting his lips. He shifted from foot to foot, like he was nervous. I suppose he was. He clearly hadn't expected me to be his client, and to my surprise it turned out that despite his poor life choices he still had some morals; like having a problem with letting the kid he used to babysit pay him for sex.

Returning to the small fridge, which I used as a makeshift seat, I studied Damian's exposed flesh in more detail while he downed his beer.

"Take the rest of your clothes off," I said.

Damian quickly drained the rest of his beer, spilling golden, foamy liquid over his chest and rounded belly, before toeing off his Vans and then shaking off his pants. He hopped around on one foot, then the other, drawing the pants and his boxers into an inside-out tangle before tossing them away onto the floor. The last thing to come off were his socks, which he bundled up and placed inside one of his shoes.

It was a beautiful sight.

Just over six foot of drug-fucked male stood stark naked in front of me. His legs were long and hairy while his cock was long and soft—as much as I'd expect from an addict. He stood in front of me, tugging his dick into a semi-stiff state, completely unembarrassed by his nakedness. That sight alone could have made me come.

"Keep wanking it," I rasped. "I wanna see how big this dick of yours really is."

He scowled but did as he was told, stroking himself to a full erection. Once he was hard, he pulled his hand away to show me my purchase. He held his arms out as if to say *what do you think?*

Not much if I were being honest.

Big D, as he'd apparently labelled himself, was in fact mediocre D. His cock was a slender six-incher, much like mine, and surrounded by coarse black hair. His balls were a good size though, low-hanging and hairy.

Sliding off my perch, I approached him slowly, to take a closer look. When I got within groping distance, I seized hold of his babymakers, plumping them in the palm of my hand. If there was one thing I had learned from my brief time as a sexually active adult it was that I enjoyed playing with a man's balls. Not only did they feel good to touch but I appreciated that in many ways they contained the essence of a male's masculinity—the ingredient to create life. My fascination with Damian's balls did not go unnoticed.

"You can suck them if you want," he suggested. "I gave my nuts a wash with a flannel before coming over."

That wasn't the seal of hygienic approval he thought it was, but I sank to the floor anyway and gave his balls a lick.

Right away I could tell they weren't as clean as they could have been, but the sweat that remained wasn't entirely unpleasant. Although only the third pair of balls I'd ever come into contact with, I knew already that each man had his own signature scent. Damian's greasy smell was more agreeable to my senses than Mr Quayle's had been but he wasn't anywhere near the heady delights of Jockey's musky nutsac.

I ran my hands up and down the black curls of his legs while I cleaned away what the flannel had missed, soaking the hair on his balls until they became matted to the wrinkly skin of his scrotum. I could hear Damian moaning lightly, perhaps enjoying this more than he'd like to let on.

Spitting his nuts out, I wrapped my lips around the head of his cock. The skin here was salty, sharp, and much less musky than what I'd just licked from his balls. I swallowed more, pushing the head of his cock deeper in my mouth. He leaked enough precum to taste, mingling with the unwashed salt of his cock.

"Bro, that feels fucking amazing." I glanced up and saw that he was pinching one of his nipples. "Keep going."

I started bobbing, moving my head up and down the shaft, slowly at first and then faster to match his breath. His hips thrust forward with each descent of my head. His hand came away from his nipple, and now it rested on the back of my head.

"Thatta boy," he sighed, running a hand through my hair. "Get some brown dick between your honky lips."

I flinched. My dick twitched.

Damian stroked my head and kept up a string of encouraging slurs, most of them racial and containing the words 'brown' or 'white' or 'honkey.' My lips went a little further down his shaft each time, until my nose was banging the tips of his unruly pubes. At first I thought his need to let me know the colour of his cock was just a kink of his, and perhaps it was, but I soon realised it was also his way of gaining control of a situation I was supposed to be leading.

Pulling away from his cock, I spluttered, "Turn around and show me your ass."

He looked down at me and a contemptuous smile played on his lips for a moment. "Don't you wanna keep sucking and get that hot Māori cum you're so desperate for?"

"No," I said firmly and returned to sit on the fridge. "I want to see the Māori ass I'm about to fuck."

He scowled once again but followed the order, turning around and showing me his ass, which was flatter than I'd hoped. His buttocks were covered in a light haze of black fur, which followed the curve toward his middle, growing thicker and darker in the crack. He leaned forward when I told him to, shoving back his hips and opening himself up with both hands.

Nice, I thought, as his asshole was pulled into a gape. In time with the beat of my heart, his anus pulsed open and closed. Knowing that was the spot my own cock would soon be entering reminded me of the enormity of this occasion. What we did in this garage would have repercussions beyond the tin walls and the rickety bed. We both knew that. The moment my cock pierced that hairy asshole my relationship with Damian would be shattered forever. He would go from being my former babysitter to being my whore. And he would always be my whore. Once was enough.

The darkness of that realisation was intoxicating, dirty, dangerous, and had me possessed by greed. I left my vantage point and walked over to him, ran a hand down the smooth muscles of his back before tickling the small patch of hair that grew just above his ass crack. The patch was loosely triangular in shape. There was a soft downy quality to the hair, and I appreciated the maleness of it.

Damian took a sharp intake of breath as my hand dipped between his cheeks, my fingers delicately prodding his hole that was moist with sweat. "I can't wait to join the list of men who have been inside here," I said.

"There's not been that many," he grumbled.

"What do most men pay you for?"

"Just to suck my cock."

"But you've been fucked before, right?"

"Yeah."

I couldn't see his face but I could tell he didn't like these questions. But that didn't stop me from asking more.

"Do you let them nut inside you?"

"I ain't got no diseases, bro, if that's what you're worried about."

"That's not what I asked. Do you let men nut inside you?"

"It's been known to happen," he replied coyly. "Not heaps, but it has."

Without warning, I reached around and shoved my fingers towards his face, "Suck," I commanded.

Damian wrapped his lips around three digits and started sucking. He moaned as he did so, putting on quite the show, as if he were sucking a cock. Finally, when I decided they were wet enough, I retrieved my spit-soaked fingers and pressed them against his sweaty hole. One by one, all three went inside.

Damian breathed heavily, growling low, never complaining. I'd never put any part of my body—fingers or cock—inside an asshole before so had nothing to compare it to. But I liked how warm he felt. Warm and slick. His sphincter offered a hugging tightness that squeezed my fingers possessively but at the same time felt like it was trying to force me back out.

Without dislodging my fingers, I stepped forward so I could see his face. Hunched over, he watched me from under heavy, half-closed eyelids. "Having fun?" he asked, all breathy.

"Yeah." I glanced down at his cock which had softened considerably. "Doesn't look like you are though."

"I'm all good. I can get him hard again when you need him."

After giving his hole one last jab, I slid my fingers free and offered them to his mouth. He opened up and sucked them clean without hesitation, his hooded eyes eyeing me seductively the entire time.

You dumb, desperate fool, I thought as I fed him the juices of his rectum on my fingers. That single act was enough to convince me that this was a man who would do absolutely anything to survive. I could only guess the depths of depravity he had dived to, the degradation he'd accepted, just to get score his next fix. The notion thrilled me. I could do anything, say anything, and this idiot would allow it.

When he'd finished sucking my fingers, I said, "Do you want to know something?"

"What's that?"

"I've never been kissed by a whore."

Damian's jaw ticked. But he got the hint. He straightened his body, turned around, and pressed his lips to mine. It was a soft and gentle peck, over within a second. "Now you have."

"So you admit you're a whore?"

"You're paying me for sex, bro, so I think we both know what that means."

"What does it mean?"

He allowed the question to hang in the air for a long time before answering. "That I'm a whore."

"A very affordable one too."

If looks could kill then I would have been on my way to the morgue in a body bag. And fair enough. The shit I was saying was beyond rude. There was an abundance of reasons why I was saying it: to assert dominance, to reclaim some of the masculinity I felt Jockey had stolen from me, to inflict some payback for the victims of Damian's violent tendencies. But the main reason, and perhaps the only reason that mattered in this moment, was that it was turning me on.

Stroking Damian's face as if he were a statue I owned, I said to him, "Now how about kissing me properly?"

He thought it over for a second, as if he had a choice, then kissed me again. This time he slipped his tongue inside my mouth, sharing with me the taste of his own ass that he'd just sucked from my fingers. While he kissed me, he lowered a hand atop my crotch, gently massaging my hardened cock through my clothes.

My hands drank of the feel of his skin beneath them as they roved along his back and shoulders, slowly angling towards the soft cleft down his spinal column. His fingers continued to grip and stroke the outline of my cock, like he was sizing me up, then I felt his hands unbuttoning my shirt.

Gently, he broke away from the kiss and started tasting the skin of my chest his hands revealed as they opened button after button. I still had the unsightly hickeys clinging to my chest from Jockey's last visit, giving me the appearance of a right slut, but Damian didn't mention them. He moaned and clamped his lips around my right nipple, his fingers teasing and twirling the hair around the left. After sucking and biting my other nipple, he headed south and sank to his knees in front of me, eye level with my crotch. His long fingers started working on my belt buckle before I'd even given him permission to go there. The leather tongue slipped loose, and the heavy buckle hung like a hinge, knocking against his hand as he popped the button on my jeans. He rose up on his knees a little, making it easier to get the zipper down. The rasp was loud, louder than the huff of my breath.

"This is the fun part of my job," he said, glancing up at me. "I always like to see what the other guy is packing."

"But I thought you were straight?"

"I am mostly, but that don't mean I ain't curious to see how I size up in comparison."

Before I could respond, he hauled my jeans and briefs down to my ankles. Cool air swirled around my nuts and licked the inside of my thighs. The sudden chill was counteracted by the warmth of Damian's breath as he leaned in to take a closer look at my cock.

It felt like there had been another power shift between us as I waited for some sort of sign that my dick was worthy enough to grace his lips.

"That figures," he said with a chuckle. "The pretty boy has a pretty dick."

"You like it then?"

"As far as dicks go you've got a pretty nice one." He looked up at me and grinned. "Trust me, bro, there are some real ugly cocks out there. I've seen enough of them."

Damian may have been *mostly* straight, but he sure as hell knew how to handle a cock. His tongue delicately circled the corona of my cock and then he took the entire shaft down his throat until his lips were at the base. Just when I thought I might be getting close to coming he pulled his mouth away and went to work on my balls, cupping them in his big hands and bringing the engorged spheres to his lips to lick and suck.

"You've got a great cock," he whispered, rubbing it against his cheek. He looked up at me. "You've got a great *everything*."

It was a hollow compliment, a tool of his trade, but it didn't take away how powerful I felt to see a man I once idolised getting acquainted with my dick. I wondered what his numerous girlfriends would think if they knew how gifted he was at pleasuring another man. Some may have found it sexy, but others would have been less impressed.

Damian closed his mouth over my cock once again and I was immediately dizzy from pleasure. I steadied myself on his broad shoulders while he gulped my dick down his throat. I was getting so close, but when I told him so Damian didn't ease up; he sucked my cock harder.

Just before he was about to flip my trigger, I pulled out and took a step back. "That's enough," I panted.

"Am I too good at that, am I?" The shit-eating grin on his face was infuriating, like he knew he had the power to make tonight come to an end prematurely.

We stayed like that for a long moment. In silence. Me standing, him on his knees.

When the threat of orgasm finally passed, I gripped my dick loosely, and slapped his cheeks with it several times. I loved the way it felt when my prick hit the heavy bones of his jaw, the way his full lips wet the sensitive skin. He opened his mouth and I let him lick just the head of my cock. When he started to close his lips around it I pulled away again.

Positioning the tip above his face, I released a thick stream of piss that splashed down over his nose and mouth. It was unexpected, and he blinked in horror, but he made no attempt to move out of the way.

"Drink," I said.

He parted his lips, allowing me to piss right into his open mouth, turning him into my own personal toilet. His mouth became filled within seconds, and I halted my flow to give him time to drink. His throat rippled as he swallowed, face grimacing as it went down.

He opened up to show me it was all gone. Saying "ahhh" as if he were at the dentist.

"Good boy," I said in the most patronising tone I could muster, then proceeded to fill his mouth up again.

We did this four times—fill, swallow, ahhh— before eventually I lost patience and just sprayed his whole face. The sight of it rushing over his face and dripping from his chin to trickle down his chest pleased me, and I moved my still-spurting dick down so that the pale yellow torrent washed his torso and soaked his cock and balls with my juice. When I was drained, I shook the last drops onto his face. The smell of it rose from the floor, where it had puddled around his knees.

"There's some on my shoes," I told him. "Lick it off."

Bending forward, he slid his tongue obediently along the piss-spattered surface of my sneakers. His ass cheeks parted as he stretched his legs wider and bowed below me, supported on his hands. His cockhead trails through the pool of urine as his face moved over my feet and he washed every drop from the canvas.

I don't think I'd ever seen anything so pathetic as this—a grown man on his knees, face and body covered in another man's piss. My piss. Maybe I would have to find a way to come up with the two grand to buy my way out of Jockey's contract, I thought. How could I be someone's submissive bitch when *I* had the power to make a grown man be my toilet. And for just fifty dollars!

Damian let out a loud burp, grimacing even more than he had when swallowing my piss. "I think it tasted better going down," he said, as if making a joke would somehow lighten the situation.

"You better get used to it because you'll be drinking way more before you leave here tonight."

He tilted his head back to look up at me, showing the vulnerable hollow of his throat. "Do you mind if I have another beer to get rid of the taste?"

I declined his request then ordered him to lie on the bed, knees into his chest and asshole open wide.

I toed off my shoes and removed my jeans that had been snagged at my ankles. Then my socks came off and I was every bit as naked as my whore. I glanced over to the bed to see Damian had followed the order; his asshole waiting for me. His legs, held apart and raised, accentuated its sacrificial vulnerability. Who knew how many men had paid for the privilege of entering his body, dozens probably, but I was confident my young cock would be the most difficult for him to accept emotionally.

I approached the bed with slow steps and grabbed one of the towels I'd laid out and used it to dry the piss from his body.

"Now finger yourself," I said. "Get your ass ready."

"Do you have any lube?"

"Yes, but you can start things off with your spit."

He muttered under his breath, something in te reo, most likely an insult. But I didn't care. I had too much power in this exchange to be worried by any petty backtalk.

After sucking on his fingers, coating them with spit, his hand snaked down between his legs, and he inserted two long fingers inside his hairy shitter. In and out they went, widening the passage for my cock. He eventually recoated his fingers with more spit before slipping them back in his hole, this time adding a third to the mix. He moaned lightly as his hole stretched to accommodate the added burn.

His brown eyes stared at me as I watched him fingering his snatch. There was a glimmer of resentment, just a hint. Unvoiced words, unexpressed emotions, were zipping between us.

After five minutes, I ordered him to pull his fingers out, and I reached under the bed for the brown bag containing the supplies.

"What's in there?" he asked.

"Condoms, lube...and a couple surprises." I waggled my eyebrows. "I think you'll enjoy them."

I retrieved the condoms and lube, opting to leave the cuffs and dildo in the bag. I wanted our first fuck to be natural, just me and him, face to face.

Placing the nozzle of the lube bottle between his ass cheeks, I squirted lube deep into his hole. The squelch it made was heavenly, as was his shivering. His hole was now a loose, juicy opening, ripe for penetration.

I put on a rubber, for my own sake rather than his, and dragged my cock down the length of his hairy trench. That made us both quiver, but for very different reasons, I imagine.

I couldn't believe it. I was just one nudge of my hips away from fucking another man. It felt like a big step for me. A way to lose another sort of virginity. Granted, my former babysitter didn't have the sexiest ass in the world, but it would do the trick.

Damian's expression softened, almost as if he wanted to hug me. He smiled at something over my shoulder and said, "What's that over there, Mike?"

I turned to take a look just before his fist came hurtling towards my face and everything went white.

I OPENED MY EYES. THE pain was so intense I shut them again. I felt something trickling on my face. I tried to wipe it, but found that I couldn't move. My eyes snapped open again. Braving the pain, I glanced around the garage and saw Damian off to the side in just his undies. My hands and feet were immovable and numb. It took only a second for bleary confusion to morph into lucid panic.

"Son of a bitch!" I cursed, pulling hard at my restraints. My wrists were cuffed to the headboard, ankles similarly bound to the footboard, all with those stupid heart-shaped love cuffs. Even as

I strained and contorted, I knew it was to no avail: the bed was sturdy as were the cuffs.

Damian strutted over. "Settle down, brother. Ain't nothing to be excited about."

"You just fucking punched me and knocked me out!"

"I didn't punch you. My fist just wanted to say hello to your face." He reached down and swiped a finger where my head thudded in pain. "It looks like it said hello a little too hard though."

I watched in horror when he pulled his finger back and saw it was covered in my blood.

"Why the fuck did you hit me?" I demanded.

"Do you really need to ask that question?" He snorted derisively. "You know you deserved a smack. Talking to me like I was a piece of shit under your shoe."

"I was just being kinky."

"No. Michael Freeman was being a naughty little boy and disrespecting me. And no little boy disrespects Damian Takarangi."

"I'm sorry. I didn't mean any of it. I was just horny."

Damian walked to the foot of the bed, disappeared from view like he was about to pick something up, then reappeared holding the dildo. Holding the girthy fake cock up to the light, his dark eyes glinted with a cold cruelty. "I'm guessing this is the surprise you said I'd like. You were fucking dreaming if you thought this was ever gonna fit inside my ass. I'm a whore, not a slut."

"I would have done it gently."

"Tell another joke, little man. You don't know the fucking meaning of gentle." He dropped the dildo onto the bed. It landed with a soft thump, rolled to rest against my calf. "You damn near ripped my ass to pieces tonight with that nasty finger-fuck business."

"Why didn't you say something?"

"Because I'm a professional," he said, sounding like he meant it. "It's my job to make you think I'm enjoying myself."

"I would have stopped if you told me to."

Unfortunately, I don't think either of us really believed that.

"I've been paid by your type plenty of times," he said.

"What type would that be?"

"The type that aren't just looking for a fuck. They're looking for control. To feel like a man by making me feel like less of one. But that ain't gonna give you what you're looking for, brother." The way he looked at me when he said that, the way his face shifted from flippant to earnest, made me think he was speaking to me out of concern.

Until...

"It never will." He tickled the sole of my foot, making me squirm. "You'll still be the same pathetic faggot afterwards."

His words hurt and infuriated. How fucking dare this piece of trash think he was better than me. But all the words of abuse I wanted to hurl back at him had to stay locked away inside my mouth. You don't argue when you're the one naked and tied to a bed.

Damian's eyes, slitted, scanned the garage. He then walked over to my discarded jeans and picked them up.

"What are you doing?"

"Looking for this," he said and pulled out my wallet. He opened it, let out a hushed "fucking hell", and then glared at me. "You lying fuck. You've got fucking hundreds in here. Hundreds! And you were only gonna pay me fifty dollars. Fifty lousy fucking dollars. You nasty little cunt."

"You're the one who agreed to that amount. No one put a gun to your head."

"I was doing you a favour because you said it was for a mate of yours."

"Now who's calling their piss rain. You agreed to that amount because you were desperate. And something tells me you've done more for less."

He didn't deny it. "And does that make what you did okay?"

"Look, I'm sorry. I'm really sorry. It was an asshole move. I know that." I shook at my restraints, rattling the bed. "Now just untie me and we can both pretend tonight never happened."

"Not so fast, boy wonder. We're renegotiating my rate before I let you go."

"Fine. Take a hundred. That's fair."

"I'm thinking I'll just take the lot to compensate for hurt feelings and all that shit."

"You can't take all of it!"

"Okay. I'll leave you the fifty dollars you were going to pay me and take the rest."

"That's still too much!"

He ignored my protest as he walked in small circles and counted out the cash. His eyes were positively glowing, like he couldn't believe his luck. He slipped one fifty dollar note back in the wallet then tucked the rest inside one of his discarded sneakers.

"That's theft if you take all that money, Damian. Theft! And you know it."

"And what, bitch? You gonna call the pigs on me and tell them the full story? Hmm? Tell them how you wanted to piss inside my mouth and bum me?" He walked back to the bed, glaring angrily.

"I don't think so. You know they ain't got time for faggots who get ripped off."

"You can't do this! It's wrong!"

"Don't worry, Mike. We've still got a couple hours left on the clock. You'll get your money's worth." He picked up the dildo and gave it a lascivious lick. "Every. Fucking. Cent."

And that's when I screamed.

Chapter 14

I SAT ON THE RED STEEL-mesh bench outside the toilets at Hickford Park. Even without an overly spanked ass, the harsh, unforgiving metal would've been incredibly uncomfortable. Tentatively, I fingered the side of my face. There was a bruise growing beneath my left eye—Damian Takarangi's calling card.

I would have cried out for help, told him to stop, but the moment I had started to scream he'd gagged me with one of his sweaty socks, stuffing my mouth full of filthy toe-cloth. He had followed that up with a piece of wide adhesive tape ripped from a roll he found on the work bench in the garage.

And that's how Damian Takarangi's payback had begun.

For the next two hours I had been at the violent thug's mercy, tied naked to a bed with no way to defend myself. While he didn't follow through on the threat of using the dildo on me, my former babysitter had taken great delight in spanking my ass until it glowed red and slapping me in the face repeatedly with the dildo.

The dildo beating had come first, whack after whack to my face with fake dick. One particular hard hit had cut my lip, feeding me the metallic taste of my own blood. Then he'd untied my feet, climbed onto the mattress and sat between my legs, before pinning my ankles behind my ears. Such a vulnerable position had my heartrate spiking and I was pretty sure I was about to be raped. Instead, he unleashed a sadistic rain of spanks down on my exposed buttocks that brought tears to my eyes and left my ass feeling like it was on fire.

As much as being spanked had hurt, it paled in comparison to the squirming pain of him tickling my feet and armpits, making me writhe and rattle the headboard to the point I'm sure I nearly broke my wrists. The tickle torture took on a more humiliating nature when he found a black sharpie pen and started graffitiing my body, head to toe, with all sorts of slurs; some of which I still hadn't managed to wash off. On my chest, written over top of my fading lovebites, there were still numerous appearances of things like *faggot, cum whore, cocksucker.* And somewhere above my ass I still bore the message *Feed my fuck hole.*

The whole time he did this, teaching me a vicious lesson, he manipulated my body like a ragdoll, holding me by the ankles to rearrange me into different positions so he could find new places of skin to mark. At one point I was practically dangling upside down so he could get to my upper back and shoulders. By the time he was done I was actually relieved to have my feet tied back to the foot of the bed. That was until the sick fuck unleashed one final act of malice: sitting his bare ass on my face and farting—twice! Much like the taste of his manky sock, the eyewatering stench would haunt me till the day I die.

It was only then that he put all his clothes back on and laughed his way out the door, leaving me tied naked to the rickety bed in the middle of the garage. I tried for hours to get my wrists free, injuring them even more. The only good thing was it wasn't Gavin who found me. It was his best mate Trent. He had turned up to borrow some of Gavin's fishing gear bright and early the following morning and got the shock of his life to find me there.

As you can imagine I was fucking mortified, but not as much as I would have been had Gavin been the one to find me. After promptly getting dressed and thanking Trent for untying me, I swore him to secrecy about the ordeal.

While the ordeal was easily the most fucking embarrassing moment of my life, I also knew that I had got off lightly. Damian could have done much, much worse.

While my face, ass and wrists hurt like a motherfucker, it was my ego that had suffered the most damage. I had been taught a sadistic lesson and reminded of my place on the hierarchy of men. Any notion I had of being an alpha male had been shredded to tiny irreparable pieces. I mean, I was clobbered and knocked about by my own dildo! How fucking embarrassing!

And to be clear, the lesson I had been taught wasn't to respect Damian, it was to be wary of the prick and to keep a safe distance. I would never respect that man. He would forever be a whore and farting sadist in my eyes. Gavin had been right about him. Damian Takarangi was bad news.

The other thing I learned, and not for the first time, was I could do with being less of an arrogant prick. While I would never approve of what Damian did, I understood why he had done it. I had been a rude shit. The fact it was born from lust was no excuse, especially because on some level I did genuinely look down my nose at Damian for whoring his ass. And if I were being honest, the truth is I had looked down on him well before ever finding out he was cruising the bogs for cash. At times I had pitied him and wanted to help him, but I don't think I could ever claim to have respected him. Maybe at some point I could forgive him enough to apologise, but today was not that day. Which is why I wasn't at Hickford Park looking for him. I was on the look out for another rent boy, the one who was being gifted the task of popping Gavin's ass cherry.

I hadn't been okay with the idea of Gavin letting Stryder fuck him, but after what had happened with Damian I felt obliged to put a stop to it. Bad boys did bad things, and while I highly doubted Gavin would find himself tied to a bed while Stryder farted on his face, Stryder was part of the bad boy tribe.

I wanted to pull my phone out, check the time, but there were only so many times I could do that before it started to look suspicious. However, the fact I had been sat on this bench for nearly an hour was suspicious in itself. Thankfully it was still a bit early before Hickford Park changed from the preferred hangout of wayward teens and became the seedy hot spot for man-on-man action. I just hoped I didn't bump into Damian while I was here. Or Mr Quayle for that matter.

Another ten minutes went by and I saw the arrival of a man who looked to be in his thirties loitering near the forested area known as the pig pen. Clearly things were about to go down any minute now. This meant it was time for me to get a wriggle on and head home. Maybe it was a sign I shouldn't be interfering with Gavin's love life.

Actually, I didn't need a sign to know that. My stepfather was a grown man capable of making his own decisions. But after my spate of recent bad ones at least one of us needed a clean track record.

As I stood up to leave, heading in the direction of home, was when I saw him. Stryder. Stood beside the fountain outside the old kiosk, he was smoking a cigarette and looking like he was on the hunt for potential clients. Approaching the fountain, I called out his name. "Stryder!"

Using a hand to block the sun out of his eyes, he peered across at me. He licked his lips and glanced around the park, seeming a little unsure of himself and hesitant about talking.

"I'm Mike. We met the other day with Gavin and Fiona." Breaking away from his gaze, I looked down at the rest of his body; his hoodie obscured his boyishly lean upper half, whilst his legs were clad in red skinny jeans, his feet fitted with a pair of Adidas trainers.

"I know who you are," he said, with a smirk. "You were the one who watched me get licked out in the toilets."

I regained my composure, almost, and said, "The reason I'm here is I wanted to ask you if—"

"What happened to your face, man?"

"Nothing. The reason I wanted to talk with you—"

"If you wanna suck me off, it'll be twenty bucks. I'll fuck you for thirty. For fifty, you can fuck me."

"What?" I glared angrily. "I didn't ask for the menu."

"The menu," he repeated, scratching his head, grin going northward. "Are you sure? Cause I suck a mean dick. And you look like you could do with a good time."

Third time lucky I thought as I tried to spit out what I wanted to say. "While I don't doubt it, the reason I'm here is to talk with you about the threesome you're planning to have with Gavin and Fiona."

"Did your dad tell you? Fiona will be pissed if he has."

"Gavin's not my dad. He's my stepdad." After that correction, I fed Stryder the teeniest of fibs. "And Gavin didn't tell me. I just overheard him on the phone speaking to Fiona about it one night."

"And?"

"And I wanted to ask if you could not do it. Just come up with an excuse or something."

"Why would I do that?"

"Because I don't think it's a good idea."

"I think it's a great idea. Fiona is hot as fuck and she said she will finger herself in front of us while we fuck."

"As alluring as that must be, I still think you need to bail on them."

He thought it over and I half-expected some grilling in return as to why I thought it was a bad idea. But it turned out Stryder had other things on his mind. "How much then?"

"How much what?"

"How much are you going to pay me to not do it."

"You can't be serious?"

"You're talking to someone who blows old dudes in a park for cash. I think you know based on that how serious I am."

"Fine," I grumbled, reaching into my pants for my wallet. I pulled out the only cash I had left. The one fifty dollar note Damian had been kind enough not to steal. "This is all I've got." I held the purple note out in front of him.

He snatched the note. "Cheers. I won't do it."

"You better fucking not," I said, trying to sound gruff and intimidating. "I'll be fucking pissed if you do."

"Calm your farm. If I give my word then you have my word."

The word of a teenage hustler didn't carry much weight in my books but it was all I could hope for. "Okay. Just don't tell them it was me who talked you out of it."

"It's all good. I'll tell them something came up. Your name won't come into it."

"If you don't mind me asking, how do you know Fiona?"

What should have been a simple response became a long-winded backstory about how Stryder's father had been Fiona's mechanic for years and that overtime the sultry blonde had become a friend of the family, even joining them on camping trips in the summer holidays. But Stryder didn't stop there, his boyish voice went on excitedly to tell me how he had two older brothers, one at university and one still living at home, and a little sister who was his favourite sibling. He shared how he'd dropped out of school twelve months ago and was having trouble looking for a job. Other than the occasional few hours helping out at his father's workshop each week, his main source of income came from blowing strangers here at Hickford Park. That then led to his admission that he thought he might be bisexual since he discovered he'd enjoyed his work in the park more than he had expected.

His mini life story was surprising. I had been thinking this sexy-mouthed hustler was the delinquent son of povo parents with bizarre taste in baby names. No, he was the delinquent son of middleclass parents who no doubt would be horrified to discover their little blond-haired angel was up to devilish deeds with strange men more than twice his age. I had wanted to cast him as a teenage villain, someone Gavin should avoid at all costs, but it seemed Stryder was just an overly-sexed dopey boy who loved football and had far less secrets than his cunning eyes suggested.

Gavin should still be avoiding him though, I thought to myself as Stryder started to tell me about the boy I'd seen him kicking a ball about with the other week.

"That's my best mate Darren. I've told him how easy it is to make money here but he won't do it. Says it's too gay."

"Having sex with men is sort of gay."

"Not when you get paid for it. And I told Darren it gets easier after a while. Even getting fucked in the ass. Hurts the first few times but after you've had a few big ones it's all good. I'm so good at it now I don't even need lube if the guy has a small dick." He smiled like his gaping asshole was a source of pride. "Everyone is really rude about the Hickford Homos but they're actually really nice. Sometimes they pay me extra for no reason."

There was so much I wanted to say to Stryder: *Just because you're getting paid for it doesn't exclude you from becoming known around town as a Hickford Homo if you get caught* and *quit being a fucking idiot and go work fulltime for your father* or *If you insist on blowing strangers for cash at least raise your fucking prices!* But it wasn't my place to say any of this. And I worried that even just having these thoughts meant I was still behaving like an arrogant shit riding a moral high horse.

When I finally was able to get a word in, I asked Stryder "So Fiona just casually came up to you one day and asked if you fancied a threeway with her and Gavin?"

Stryder nodded like it wasn't a big deal. "It's not the first time. I've been banged by her last two boyfriends. This time though your stepdad was gonna take the bottom bunk. I was sort of looking forward to it. Fiona made him show me his ass the other day at your house and it looked more than fuckable."

Trying to block out images of Gavin mooning Stryder, I asked, "Did you just say Fiona's *last two boyfriends*?"

"Yeah."

"Was one of them called Jockey by any chance?"

"I think so." Stryder nodded eagerly. "Are you talking about that weird dude who dresses up like he's in the army?"

"That's the one."

He laughed. "Yeah, he was one of them. I could barely walk the next day after him. He might look like a skinny runt but that dude has a machine gun cock." Stryder pretended to be holding a weapon and did the sound effects for me. "*Pow. Pow. Pow.*"

My asshole tingled.

When he put his imaginary gun down, he said, "I'm guessing that's who will take my place when I tell Fiona I can't do the threeway."

"Excuse me?"

"She said when she asked me that if I couldn't do it then she'd ask one of her exes. I'm picking she was talking about army boy. I pity your stepdad's asshole if that's the case. At least I'd leave him being able to walk the next day." Before I had a chance to question him any further, Stryder spotted a businessman getting out of his car. "Gotta go. Cheers for the fiddy."

I watched him speed-walk towards the new arrival as I stood there wondering if I had just made shit a whole lot worse.

Chapter 15

"WHAT HAPPENED TO YOUR face?"

I looked up from my phone, surprised to see Gavin home from work already. Standing in front of the couch where I sat, he wore an expression that was hovering somewhere between curious and concerned.

"The wind changed," I said.

"I'm being serious, Mike." He walked closer and smoothed my long hair back so he could get a closer look at the damage. "It looks sore. Do you need me to take you to the hospital?"

"I don't need the hospital to prescribe me pain killers. We have them in the cupboard."

"What if you have concussion? This looks nasty."

"I'm fine. Honest."

Gavin was an affectionate mother goose type when someone he cared about was in pain, so I wasn't surprised when he leaned down to kiss my forehead. "Let me know if you change your mind. Head injuries can be serious, kiddo."

I nodded, suddenly choked up, reminded of things I didn't want to think about. Like how this man was my only support network. And how, after four years of it just being the two of us, I was on the verge of being replaced by Fiona's children.

Gavin returned to stand the other side of the coffee table. "Are you going to tell me what happened?"

"Long story short: it was an accident."

He raised an eyebrow. "This accident wouldn't have anything to do with you being found tied naked to a bed in the garage, would it?"

"That chubby fucker," I hissed. "I told Trent to keep his mouth shut."

"Don't be mad at Trent. He only told me because he was concerned. He said your face was covered in blood."

"It wasn't that bad."

"Are you sure? Because one side of your face looks like it's been used as a punching bag." He shook his head. "And naked? Tied to the bed?"

Being the overly analytical sod that I am, I had prepared for the event of Trent having a big fucking mouth. "It was a stupid dare I did for Jockey. As a belated birthday present. Me, him and Brian do them every year."

"What in the flying fuck was this dare?"

"It was to be tied naked to a bed and see if I could do a Houdini and untie myself before you got home."

"That doesn't explain why your face is so injured."

"It does when you take into account how drunk I got to do the dare in the first place. I tripped and hit my face before Jockey tied me up."

His eyes turned to slits, distrustful. "And Jockey still expected you to do the dare even though you were covered in blood?"

"He was drunk too. Really drunk."

"But what about the sexy vampire? I thought the reason I was going out last night was so you could have him stay over?"

"He cancelled."

Gavin took his time to absorb the bullshit he was being fed. It was only when he started to smile that I calmed down. "You boys are fucking crazy with these dares. I hope when it's your birthday you make sure Jockey returns the favour."

"I'm sure I'll think of something," I said. "Anyway, can we just pretend it never happened. It's fucking embarrassing."

Gavin grinned. "According to Trent you got nothing to be embarrassed about."

"Trent told you about my cock?"

"No. He just said he wished he had a body like yours. He reckons you're in real good shape." Gavin's grin widened. "No homo, homo."

I barked a laugh, face burning, but fought to keep my tone aloof. "Very funny."

"I can make that joke, right?"

"Yes, Gavin. You can make that joke."

A comfortable silence settled over us and Gavin's eyes did that thoughtful, faraway thing, scanning my face, and he blew air through his lips.

"Come to think of it," he said, "Trent must have had a good geeze at your business while untying the knots because he reckons after seeing you naked, he's decided to start shaving his balls. Apparently you've got a very aesthetically pleasing ball bag. Now that's high praise considering how fucking ugly most men's balls are."

My cheeks, already warm from the bruising, began to get scorching hot while Gavin laughed. I suppose it was a compliment, sort of, but it was an embarrassing one.

"I trim the old bush on occasion," Gavin said, "but can't say I've gone in with the razor to shave my nuts yet. I'm always worried I might cut the fuckers off."

"Unless it's Sweeny Todd shaving them I think you'll be fine."

Gavin was about to respond but stopped abruptly when he saw me prop my bare feet up onto the coffee table.

"Don't lecture me about putting my feet on here," I said, pre-empting a lecture. "You do it all the time."

With the most coy of expressions, Gavin replied, "Has Jockey met your sexy vampire?"

"No."

"But he knows who he is, right?"

My pulse sped up. What did he know? Had Jockey said something to Fiona that had got passed on.

"Unless..." Gavin began in a conspiratorial whisper, "Jockey is the sexy vampire."

My slack-jawed face and gaping mouth must have screamed guilt but Gavin just laughed.

"Could you imagine that," he said. "You and Jockey. Together? That would be one for the joke book. Thankfully I know you're not that stupid to date a Savage. And unfortunately I know all too well from Fiona how much of a pussy hound Jockey is. Nothing against the guy, he's always been a good mate to you, much better than that Brian prick, but you gotta admit that Jockey is a bit of a dopey fucker. It still baffles the fuck out of me that Fiona ever dated the guy. Surely she'd heard about him being a bit...special shall we say. The whole family is. Don't get me wrong, I love me some white trash. Fun people. But that Savage bunch are just one sibling marriage away from being the hills have eyes."

Many in town shared Gavin's view of the Savage family. They were a special breed. Which is why my having signed a master slave contract with Jockey would be the kiss of death for my already less than stella reputation.

"Just between you and me," Gavin continued, "I sort of wish Jockey was gay so I wouldn't have to worry about him trying to get back with Fiona."

"You don't have to worry about that. Jockey's moved on."

"That's what Fiona reckons but it never hurts to be mindful of the competition. And in my experience exes are always competition. A man's gotta match the performance of the fella who came before him. Normally I'm not bothered by that sort of shit, ya know? I've always been confident in my ability to please a woman, but Jockey's a young lad in his prime, loads of energy, cum for days, which can be a bit daunting for an older dog like me. Obviously I'm not some old geezer needing a script for Viagra but my turnaround time ain't what it used to be, if you know what I mean."

While I did not need a front row seat to Gavin giving a speech about his sexual stamina, I was actually quite pleased he was making this about himself. It averted the disaster of Jockey being outed as my sexy vampire.

I zoned out as Gavin prattled on about his ability to please a woman, but he wrangled me back to the conversation when he said, "Jockey knows him though, right?"

"Knows who?"

"Your sexy vampire."

"Um...Jockey knows *of* him."

"And I'm guessing you've been telling Jockey stories about what you and this mystery man get up to?"

"Uh..."

"You know you can tell me those sorts of stories too, right? I don't care if you're boning a dude. Sex stories are fun. That's why I share mine."

"Okay?"

"Cool. At least I know you got good taste in men." He waggled his eyebrows. "I'm often told how good us Māori boys are in the sack."

"What are you on about?"

"Your feet," he said, and pointed at them.

"I raised my left foot in the air and wiggled my toes. "It's just a foot, Gavin. I've got two of them."

"Look underneath, genius."

I leaned forward and looked at the sole of my foot. My heart flipped like Tom Daley diving for gold. In faded black, but still easily readable, was the message: *I suck nigga cock.* I quickly checked under my other foot and found another one. *This whitey loves Māori cum.*

"Oh god...I-I didn't know they were there."

"Don't sweat it, *whitey.*" Gavin sniggered like a dirty school boy. "I think it's funny. But you may not want to leave the house without shoes on. You're the minority in this neighbourhood and some of us niggers might find it offensive."

"I'm not the one who wrote it! I'd never call someone that. Honest."

"I know. I'm just teasing ya." Gavin knelt down and stroked the foot telling the world I love Māori cum. "This one isn't so bad. It might even make you popular. Most men love a swallower."

"Good to know," I groaned sarcastically. "Maybe next time I'll get it written on my forehead."

Gavin smiled, still studying the bottom of my foot. "I'm not sure what it's like in the gay world but I can tell you it is hard to find a woman who doesn't run to the sink to spit that shit right out. Fiona's a right vixen in the sac and even she doesn't like swallowing."

"If you're looking for someone to swallow then you might want to consider switching teams." It was meant as a joke but came out way more suggestive than I intended.

"Of course you'd say that." Gavin stroked my foot again. "After all, you're the one who *luuurves* Māori cum."

The surge in humiliation had me nearly curse the culprit's name out loud. "Fucking Dami—" I stopped myself just in time. "I'm gonna kill Jockey when I see him next."

Gavin chuckled, still smiling at the shameful scribble on my foot. "Random, but has anyone ever told you you've got nice feet?" He then blew on the underside of my toes.

The compliment was so leftfield that I actually responded honestly. "Yeah. My sexy vampire is particularly fond of them."

"I can see why. They're kinda sexy...for smelly boy feet." His gaze slowly drifted from my feet to my face as he smiled and said, "No homo, *homo*."

"You better stop teasing me or I might come after your Māori cum."

Gavin grinned, unabashed, and squeezed my foot. "Just so you know, that's not quite the threat you think it is." With a laugh, he rose to his full height and left the room.

I laughed too because he was joking.

Wasn't he?

Chapter 16

THE SIZZLE OF MEAT hitting a grill crackled through the café's kitchen, followed closely by the aromas of olive oil and warm, freshly baked bread. My stomach rumbled, and I pressed a hand over my abdomen. This was the problem working in the kitchen, I was always getting hungry from the wonderful smells. The only time food smelled this good at home was when Gavin or I bought takeout home.

Unfortunately I didn't have much choice about spending my entire shift helping in the kitchen today. Carol had decided my bruised face was too much of a distraction for me to help out on the counter. Naturally all my coworkers had quizzed me about my cut lip and blackeye but they'd seemed happy enough to believe my bullshit story about falling off a scooter.

Today's shift had been an early start for me which meant I got to finish at four o'clock when Chad arrived to take over as manager for the late shift when the café would transform into bar mode. I had previously viewed Carol's tall hipster son as a total fuck-knuckle whose presence grated my nerves, but now I genuinely enjoyed working closing shifts with him and was a bit disappointed when he walked in just as I was finishing up for the day—but not disappointed enough to hang around chatting with him if I wasn't being paid.

Releasing my greasy hair from the manbun it had been tied in, I strolled along the main street in search of an ATM to see if last week's wages had been deposited into my bank account. The money was in there and I took out some cash so I could pay Gavin my board when I got home. The sound of the machine coughing out three twenty-dollar notes was exciting but far too short-lived.

Pay day was always a reminder as to how povo my existence actually was. My earnings were miniscule, like 99% of hospo workers, and I sometimes wondered if I'd be better off just going onto the benefit. The majority of adults in my neighbourhood received a benefit of some kind. I had grown up in one of the few household exceptions thanks to Mum and Gavin's strong work ethics, which is probably why I resisted the temptation of joining the cult of jobless youth. Another reason I was hesitant to join the dole queue was the mind-numbing seminars I had heard the unemployed had to attend. Jockey, who'd been between jobs a couple years back, had been to one such seminar where a young, well-spoken government employee had explained to her disinterested audience the importance of wearing matching shoes to job interviews. The spooky part about that was Jockey reckoned this chick wasn't even taking the piss—she genuinely thought the down and out were that fucking stupid.

Screw that, I thought. I would just have to tolerate my job's low wages and rude customers until I decided what it was I wanted to do with my life. I still had no idea. No plan as to how I was going to ever leave my shitty town. My only aspiration was to write the next great Kiwi novel, and that was about as realistic as Damian Takarangi returning the money he'd stolen from me.

My hands formed fists at the memory of Damian getting the better of me—his hateful words 'you'll still just be a pathetic faggot' were burned onto my brain. It made my chest literally ache. And I kind of wanted to break every shop window I passed. But that wouldn't achieve anything. As much as it pained me, I knew this was one of those times where I just had to accept defeat.

Beneath my anger at my former babysitter was a begrudging sort of gratitude for what he'd done. Damian's nasty stunt had cured any foolish notion I'd been having that signing Jockey's contract had been a mistake. I suppose a part of me had been under the illusion that I had only signed Jockey's contract out of necessity, and that secretly I was still the superior in our friendship. I think that had been easier for my ego to deal with than acknowledging what Jockey had said all along—that I was an inferior male. Well, I certainly felt inferior right now. If I couldn't take control of a sexual situation I was paying for then I had no right to think of myself as Jockey's superior.

Reinforcing this less than welcome self-admission of mine was the Hierarchy website Jockey had recommended I check out. I'd stayed up late last night diving deeper into the site, researching the twisted philosophy my new owner bought into so heavily. The site was a wealth of information, much of which I was tempted to write off as bullshit, but I'd be lying if I didn't say it was fascinating. Maybe there really was a benefit for guys like myself to admit their lowly place on the hierarchy and assume the position at the feet of more worthy men. The site preached that happiness could only be found when an individual was fulfilling their role and respecting their true nature.

Brushing that unwanted truth aside, I let my mind wander to my other problem: Gavin.

Tonight was the night he was supposed to be having a threeway with Fiona and Stryder. The plan was he would go straight to Fiona's house after work where he would be unlocked and cleaned and made presentable for his teenage lover. I'd been told all about it this morning at breakfast as Gavi excitedly explained how good it would feel to stop wearing the cock cage.

"I can't tell you how fucking good it will feel to have a piss standing up again," he had said. "I think that's what I've missed the most. Other than the sex, of course."

I'd had to smile and nod to an endless supply of jokes about his cock's impending freedom while I sat there secretly stewing about Stryder. The snot-faced weasel clearly hadn't cancelled yet which meant it was starting to look like I'd been ripped off by yet another Hickford Park hustler.

If this threeway went ahead, which it looked an awful fucking lot like it would, then it was official: Gavin Masters was a fucking moron! It would also confirm just how into Fiona the man was. But I'd sort of figured that out the moment he told me he was even considering the threeway. It was one thing for Gavin to recite tales of his drunken youth where he'd laugh and joke about making out with Trent at parties, but this threeway was the real deal, and it wouldn't just be some sloppy-face smooches. Before the night was over Gavin would be the owner of a fucked asshole and his lips would know what a cock tasted like.

It shouldn't have bugged me so much but I couldn't control this protective instinct I had towards Gavin. Just like I had been his main priority for the past four years, he had also been mine.

My foul mood wasn't helped when I got home and saw how messy the place was. The kitchen and lounge had looked just as bad this morning but I'd been too focused on getting ready for work to be bothered by the mess. Now though it bugged me and I knew that if one of us didn't do the dishes soon we wouldn't have any clean plates or cups left. This was a common occurrence when two men with an aversion to cleaning lived together. Gavin and I didn't have a set roster and sort of relied on the other to be in the mood to clean. Needless to say that wasn't the most efficient cleaning system and more often than not our kitchen bench resembled a cluttered boardgame. But as I stood there scowling at the mess, and realising there was also a foul smell accompanying it, I realised this week we had been particularly neglectful. It was safe to assume we'd both been more concerned with other things than the slowly festering mess emanating from the kitchen bench.

I hunted through the dishes to try and find the offending smell. It was right at the bottom growing from a plate of leftover chicken nuggets that had started sprouting grey furry mould. If the mould had legs you could have sworn it was a dead cat.

"That's fucking gross," I said, covering it back up with the other plates.

The sensible thing to do would have been to fill the sink with hot water and make a start at cleaning but I opted instead to go get changed out of my work clothes, promising myself to do the dishes before bed.

When I wandered into my bedroom I saw that Gavin must have checked the mailbox before leaving for work because there was a postcard waiting for me on my study desk. Knowing it would be from my mother, I approached the glossy postcard with about as much enthusiasm as I would walking into a kick in the nuts.

On the front was a mosaic of Cairns and tropical rainforests. Written on the back was a short little note that didn't say much at all, as per usual.

Thinking of you. Ricky and I are holidaying in Cairns for a few days before we move up to Darwin. I'm very excited to see our new house. I miss you.
Love Mum xxx

I rolled my eyes and placed the postcard in a drawer with the others she had sent me through the years. Each time Mum wrote me was usually just to let me know her and Ricky were on the move again. The pair's constant moving had less to do with adventure than it did with Ricky's inability to hold down a job. That's what Gavin had said. I agreed with him though. Back here in New Zealand Ricky had been able to rely on the unemployment benefit between jobs, but Australia wasn't so generous when it came to jobless Kiwis. Deemed the lucky country, Australia offered better money, better nightlife, better weather, better lots of things... but in many ways New Zealanders were treated like second class citizens over there, which is why the thought of joining Mum had never appealed to me.

Well, that and the fact she had never asked me to.

I returned to the kitchen where I used the last clean bowl in the house to make myself a snack of two-minute noodles. Avoiding casting my gaze at the dirty dishes, I took the bowl of noodles with me through to the lounge and switched on the television. There was nothing decent on so I settled on watching some show about a family living rough in Alaska. Man versus wild shit held little interest for me but at least one of the guys was sort of hot so I perved at him while I slurped up the tasty beef noodles.

All too soon the programme came to an end and was replaced by some home renovation show which was void of any eye candy.

"Fucking typical," I grumbled.

I'd barely been home ten minutes and I was already bored shitless. It was moments like these that reminded me of Brian and how not all that long ago I had had a best friend to call and hangout with every day of the week.

Not anymore.

To be honest, I had thought I might have heard from the four-eyed snob after my shitty text to him the other day. But no. Nothing. He was if nothing else consistent.

As I sat there half-watching the home renovation show, I wondered what Brian would think if he knew what I'd become. That I'd allowed myself to become an owned faggot. While I'm sure the conservative twat would be horrified to hear I was about to begin a twelve-month period of being fucked most days by another man, I think he would have been more horrified to know whose cock would be fucking me.

Jockey had always been a joke to Brian, and there had been two times Brian had suggested we seriously consider distancing ourselves from the redneck stoner. But each time something had happened to make Jockey useful in Brian's eyes. The first time had been when Jockey, who was two-and-a-bit years older than us, turned eighteen and Brian suddenly realised it meant we had someone to buy us beer. But that novelty wore off when Brian's cousin turned eighteen a year later and once again my best mate was suggesting we give Jockey the flick. Once again though something happened that changed Brian's tune.

Fiona Bachelor.

When Jockey first told us he'd got a girlfriend with kids, Brian and I had pissed ourselves laughing. That was until Jockey introduced us to his new girlfriend and we saw how pretty she was. Brian had been especially impressed, and I suspect may have had a crush on Fiona himself. That ended any talk of ditching Jockey with Brian telling me that Fiona might have some hot friends that also fancied younger men. This turned out to be wishful thinking because after introducing us to Fiona, Jockey made sure to keep his time with mates and his girlfriend separate.

Switching off the television, I decided it was time to tackles those dishes. But before I did that, I decided to be nosey and check out Brian's Instagram. I hadn't stalked his social media for days now, not since I'd realised that looking at pictures of him only left me sad—and a little horny. But fuck it, I thought. The Alaska dude had already got me horny so why not let Brian finish the job. Jizzing on Brian's screen-trapped face would perk me up.

As I tapped on the Instagram logo on my phone to sign in, I saw that I had a new follower: *Damian Takarangi.*

Shaking my head, I laughed in shock. I couldn't believe the dude who'd beaten me with a dildo, and then mugged me, had the audacity to follow me online. "You're fucking dreaming if you think I'll return the follow, ass-wipe."

I wondered why the hell Damian thought this would be a good thing to do. Did he think it was funny? Or had he done it as a threat? A way to let me know I should keep my mouth shut. He needn't worry about me snitching. There was no way on this earth I would be going to the police to explain what had happened.

Ignoring Damian's random follow, I typed in Brian's name to see if he had any new pics up. I was hoping the four-eyed stud might have posted some new shirtless shots of himself, maybe some from a toga party. Uni students did that sort of shit, right?

The search came back *No users found.* Assuming I'd mistyped his name, I tried looking for him again. Still no user found. I stared at my phone in disbelief.

"The fucker blocked me!"

Chapter 17

NUMBNESS.

That's what had hit me first.

I felt disconnected from the world, as if someone had put a snow globe over me. In fact, I was so numb after learning that Brian had blocked me that I'd calmly walked into the kitchen and washed all the dishes. I was still numb an hour later when I decided to go for a walk. I'd gone to visit Jockey first but he was out. Rather than return home I carried on walking and slowly, bit by bit, the numbness left me until I was able to feel the seething rage bubbling away inside me.

I continued walking—walking like I had somewhere to be. But in reality, I didn't have to be anywhere, and I really didn't need to be headed directly to Hickford Park. But that was the direction my feet were taking me and in the back of my mind I knew the reason for this. It repulsed me, and made me shake with anger, but still I kept walking. Walking towards the only form of revenge I felt I had at my disposal.

I was going to fuck Mr Quayle.

The thought of sticking my dick inside a man his age was grim, but it was a sacrifice my cock was willing to make. Every thrust of my hips would be a *fuck you* to my former best friend. Even if I never told Brian what I'd done it would still fill me with satisfaction to know I had ass-fucked the man he looked up to most in this world.

Not only was I angry but I felt like a fool. And if there was one thing I hated it was being made to look stupid. And I was definitely guilty of being stupid for not blocking Brian first. The dude had been ignoring me for weeks now so I should have known this was coming. At least if I'd had the sense to block him first then I would have felt like I'd had some active part in the end of our friendship. Instead I had been the dumb idiot who'd sat at home waiting patiently for him to get in touch, making excuses for his silence well longer than I should have.

I'll tell you what won't be silent, Brian. Me fucking your dad's asshole.

My dick started hardening in anticipation of the sadistic fuck I was about to dish out. It didn't matter this would be my first time topping, and therefore lacking experience, I had faith in my rage to follow through on the most delicious of hatefucks. I would fuck Mr Quayle until either his hole or my dick was dripping blood. This was not going to be a good time for Brian's old man, but Rowan Quayle would be all too keen to drop his pants for my young cock. And if he wanted my young cock—which he would—then he would have no choice but to splash out for a hotel room where we could fuck in private.

It was well and truly dark by the time I reached Hickford Park and I finally got to see just how busy the place got when the sun went down. There must have been close to twenty cars parked up, and that wasn't including the men who would have parked a few blocks away in an effort to be more discreet. Add to that the men who would have walked or cycled here then it became quite obvious how many Hickford Homos there were in this town. I wondered how many of the men here tonight had been unlucky enough to be captured on video by the homophobe vigilante. That was perhaps the only thing that made me cautious about entering the park at this hour; the fear of being captured on film and finding myself on that website Jockey had made me look up. That, and stumbling across Moose the skinhead and his freakishly big cock.

The first dude I saw was a beefy-looking bloke about forty. He winked at me as I walked past. I ignored the wink and he then said, "Fancy some fun, fella?" I ignored him again and kept on walking.

This happened four more times; passing older men who winked or hollered some sort of come on. One of them must have thought rather highly of himself cause after I ignored him he called out "fuck you ya stuck-up prick."

My search for Brian's father wasn't as easy as I had assumed it would be. I'd thought I would find him loitering near the toilets, or maybe over by the old kiosk with the hustlers, but he wasn't in either of those two places. I zigged and zagged my way across the grassy domain, wandering if he was one of the floating figures wandering aimlessly across the field. After about fifteen minutes of searching, my sneakers and jeans damp from the dew-soaked grass, I was just about ready to give up and go back home.

But there was one last place I hadn't yet checked.

The pig pen.

The thought of venturing there in the dark left me uneasy, especially after the stories Damian had told me. But that was the only place Rowan could be, and if I wanted revenge then I would just have to be a big boy and go look.

In sluggish steps, I made my way towards the sloping hill where the small patch of forest played host to the more depraved antics of

Hickford Park's visitors. I got to the tree-line and stopped abruptly when I heard moaning. I peered into the gloom of the trees, jerking my head about like a sparrow watching for a cat. It went quiet and I thought maybe I had imagined it.

Then the moaning returned, shaped now into a definite voice. A man's voice. More a groan than a moan. There was fear in it. Maybe pleading. Maybe pain. A chilly patch of gooseflesh crinkled at the back of my neck and slithered down my spine.

"Fuck the bitch, Vinnie," I heard someone say. "Rape its pussy."

Rape?

Suddenly concerned, I forced myself to enter the darkened woods, worried what I might find. I only made it a few steps before I heard the person moaning cry out, in a much more enthusiastic tone, "Fuck me, Daddy! Fuck my mangina!"

Raucous laughter followed.

That answered a couple questions. A; there was at least four or five people up there, and B; whatever was happening was consensual. Fucked up for sure, but consensual.

From where I was standing I could make out the glow of a torch or some kind of light coming from the top of the small slope. It was up there, in a small clearing where I had taken a piss the other week, that the action was going down. The night air was a symphony of flesh slapping against flesh, vicious grunts and desperate moans. The pig being fucked continued to wail loudly, begging for more dick. I couldn't be sure how many men were involved but my guess was at least five judging by the different tones of laughter I heard.

Propelled by a curiosity I should have stayed away from, I continued my way up the small hill until I came to the edge of the clearing and saw what could only be described as kinky ingenuity.

Hanging from the branch of a tree was a large torch acting as a makeshift spotlight. Its beam glowed down on a naked man tied to a low, padded sawhorse. He was bent lengthwise over it with his four limbs fastened to each of the legs. His face was covered by a black gimp mask. A shock of scraggly brown hair was slipped out the back of the mask and dangling over his neck, suggesting the dude had a mullet hairdo. It was hard to gauge his age without seeing his face but his pale body looked to be in reasonable shape; broad shoulders, strong biceps and well-defined legs covered with dark, masculine curly hairs that trailed from his thighs right down to his ankles.

At the head of the sawhorse stood a pudgy bald man rubbing his balls on the naked man's masked face while at the other end a young Indian man wearing a turban—whom I assumed must be Vinnie—rutted the naked man's asshole. Vinnie was handsome and I found myself wishing he'd taken his clothes off for the fuck, but all he'd done apparently was unzip and flop his cock out. Clearly this was a minimal effort fuck for him.

A group of about seven men stood around the sawhorse trio, watching and cheering. Their ages varied but most appeared to be middle-aged and older. And none were attractive like Vinnie.

I held back a few metres, safely hidden amongst the darkness of the trees. I worried that my presence wasn't wanted here. But more worried that it might be. While the naked dude was clearly getting off on being used like a fuck-sleeve, I could not imagine anything worse than being restrained, spread-eagled and utterly helpless.

I noticed that the legs of the sawhorse had ropes attached; each one pulled taut and tied to pegs in the ground to ensure the device was steady. Near one of the pegs was a pile of clothes.

Aside from being shocked at the depravity unfolding in front of me, I was mostly impressed at the effort someone had gone to in creating this outdoor freakshow.

None of the men here were Mr Quayle and I told myself I should get a move on and look elsewhere for Brian's father, but my dick had other ideas. It liked what it saw. It urged me to step forward and take a closer look, maybe even join in. Thankfully I still had enough blood flowing through my big brain to not be so stupid.

Vinnie suddenly jerked his head back, like he'd just been punched between the shoulder blades, and let out a loud, deep roar. "Here it comes, piggy. Your reward."

"Fuck yeah!" the pig shouted as if he'd just scored a touchdown. "Feed me that cum!" His hyper masculine outburst was swiftly followed by a satisfied gasp as Vinnie must have emptied his balls inside him.

The men all clapped as Vinnie pulled his bare cock out of the man's hole and gave his rump a hard slap.

"Who's wants to fuck the pig next?" Vinnie asked as he turned to face the spectators, his soiled cock hanging out the front of his fly.

"I'll have a go at it," said a voice in the crowd, and a scrawny man with a weathered face and short, spiky grey hair came forward.

The man quickly undid his khaki slacks and slipped them down around his hairy knees. His penis flopped onto his thigh as it was released; it was long, thin and furiously red. Despite his age—which I guessed to be about fifty—he tugged his flaccid cock to a fully-hard state as quickly as a man half his age. He positioned his cock at the mouth of the pig's asshole, then drove the shaft all the way home with a single gut-wrenching thrust.

The pig jolted so hard that the loose strands of his mullet bounced over his neck. The man behind him promptly pulled his cock all the way out, then speared the pig's ass to the hilt again, matching the pig's high-pitched squeal with a grunt.

He grabbed the pig's hips and began to pump at a leisurely pace, looking like he was settling in for a long, hard screw. The pig's shrieking subsided to a breathless whimper through gritted teeth. "Yes—Daddy—please. Fuck me—fuck me, Daddy."

As the pig adjusted to having a new man inside his shitter, he started tonguing the tip of the bald man's cock. His moaning soon returned when his ass began to get screwed with brutal force. The scrawny dude rooting him spanked his ass like he was whipping a horse. It had to hurt. Now and then the pig would yelp "You're too rough" or "Stop! It's hurting" but the scrawny dude just kept fucking him ruthlessly and the pig would eventually giggle, like he found his own lack of consent a joke.

Mullet man is off his fucking rocker, I decided.

"Where did you find this slut?" one of the men in the crowd asked the Vinnie guy.

"Grindr," Vinnie replied. "He said he had a daddy fantasy so I told him I knew where to find loads of daddies."

"The bitch sure knows how to take a cock," interjected the man doing the fucking.

"He reckons he's straight and on the downlow," Vinnie said, his Punjabi accent laced with derision. "So he probably practices at home using his wife's dildo."

Someone in the crowd snorted and said, "If I was married to a man with such a small cock I'd own a dildo too."

The men all laughed, including the pig even though the joke was at his expense. But then, as if his brain was on some sort of delay, he spat the bald man's dick out and said, "Fuck you, cunts! My dick ain't small. Faggots."

This just made the men laugh even more. I also found it funny considering the pig was the last person to be calling anyone a faggot.

"Fuck this," the pig snapped. "Untie me. I'm over it."

The dude fucking him gave his ass a hard slap and told him "Settle down, sonny. Daddy ain't finished using your fuck-hole yet."

The mask concealed the emotion on the pig's face but judging by the white knuckles of his clenched fists it was safe to say he was fucking furious. I waited for him to scream abuse, demanding to be let go, but what came out was an effeminate squeal, so different to his normal speaking voice, and he cried out, "Fuck me, Daddy! Fuck my mangina!"

The men all laughed and the pig returned his lips to the bald man's dick.

"This dude is seriously fucked in the head," I whispered to myself.

"That's what drugs can do to a man, Mike."

Who said that?

Startled, I turned around to see a shadowy figure approaching me from behind. I couldn't make out his face but I could see he was wearing baggy jeans and a leather jacket. It was only when he came to a standstill right in front of me that I realised all too late who it was. Cold sweat slimed my skin, and my heart thumped. I opened my mouth to say his name but it got stuck in my throat. *Damian...*

Chapter 18

DAMIAN LOOKED ME UP and down with a goofy grin and an unfocused eye. He'd clearly had a few. If his droopy face muscles weren't enough to give away his pissed state then his alcohol-laced breath certainly was.

"I thought I told you this isn't the sort of place for nice boys to visit." His tone was sinister and the goofy grin vanished. "But then I did learn the other night that you're not a very nice boy. Are you, Mike?" He reached out, grabbing my groin through my pants. I gasped, and flushed, and felt myself twitch.

"Let go of me," I whisper-shouted, not wanting to alert the men to our presence.

Damian squeezed my balls a little tighter, not painfully so, but enough to let me know he had a good grip on me. "Why should I? You're obviously here looking for trouble and now you've found it."

"I didn't come here looking for trouble. Or you. Honest."

He studied my face intently, searching for any hint of a lie. He gave my nuts one last squeeze then let go. "Then what are you doing here?"

"No reason. I'm just out for a walk."

"You don't go out for a walk in Hickford Park. So what are you really doing here?"

"I'm looking for someone. Not you. Someone else."

"Who?"

Feeling brave—after taking a step back— I replied, "That's none of your business."

"Aw, why you being so rude?"

"Because you assaulted me and stole my fucking money."

"I didn't steal nothing from you. Just took what I was owed."

"Whatever," I grumbled.

"If it makes you feel better I did feel a bit guilty about it the next day. That's why I followed you on Instagram. Did you see? That was my way of saying sorry."

"You can say sorry by giving me my money back."

He laughed then, like I'd said something dumb. "That cash is long gone, brother. Hence I'm out here tonight to try and make some more moolah." He reached into his pocket and pulled out a packet of cigarettes. Cigarettes my money had probably paid for. "I bet that turns you on, don't it? Me out here being a whore. Selling my dick for cash. Fuck, you couldn't remind me enough about what I do the other night."

I didn't appreciate him using my desire against me like this. "I was horny. Sue me."

He lit a cigarette and took deep inhale then let the smoke waft in my direction. His drug-fucked gaze narrowed, pinning me to the spot where I stood. I wanted to leave, get away from the thuggish prick, but I didn't fancy walking past him any more than I fancied walking the other direction and outing my presence to the horny fuckers raping the pig.

I was trapped.

"You know," Damian said on an exhale of smoke, "I never would have thought that the sweet little boy I used to babysit would grow up to be a faggot."

"And I never thought my cool babysitter would end up having a prolapsed asshole from whoring at Hickford Park. But here we are."

He laughed. "My ass ain't loose, brother. I keep my shit tight."

"I guess I'd know that if you hadn't been a fucking psycho and assaulted me right before I was about to fuck you."

"If you flick me twenty bucks you can still find out."

It was my turn to laugh. "Somebody's dropped their price a bit since they came to my house."

"That's because you wanted a four-hour session with kink. This is just a quick scuttle in the bushes."

"Gosh, when you put it like that...the answer is still *no*."

"Don't be a dick, oi. Just throw me twenty bucks." He quickly sweetened his voice and added, "You can call me a whore while you fuck me if you want."

Damian followed the offer up with a sheepish grin. I should've replied with a fist to the face, just like I should've not bothered coming here tonight. But then I thought of Damian's furry ass and all the fun I could have with it, and before I knew it my hand was itching to grab my wallet. My cock didn't hold a grudge.

But thankfully I had enough self-respect to not pull my wallet out. "I'm not fucking you, Damian."

"Why not?"

"For starters, you assaulted me and stole my money."

"I already said I was sorry."

"That still doesn't change the fact that I don't want to become a Hickford Homo. *Like you*." That venomous jab was the closest to a punch I could swing. "And even just a quick scuttle in these bushes will give me a label I'd rather not have."

"If you're worried about the nutter who used to come here with the camera then don't be. That prick is long gone. Ain't no one gonna know."

"I would know," I said haughtily.

Damian opened his mouth to respond but he was cut off by the men behind us who let out a raucous round of laughter. I turned around to see the bald man was pissing in the pig's masked face. The men watching all laughed as the pig thrashed about on the sawhorse. Though he was not overly muscled, the pig was clearly athletic. Every line of muscle was taut and flexing as he struggled against his restraints. But it was no use. He was getting a piss facial if he liked it or not.

Just as the bald man finished his piss, the scrawny dude at the rear announced to everyone he was "about to fill this bitch." Similar to Vinnie before him, when the scrawny dude finished ejaculating, he pulled out of the pig's ass, gave his ass cheeks a smack, and walked away.

I nearly let out a squawk when I felt wet lips kiss the back of my neck.

Damian whispered in my ear. "I'm so horny for a fuck." He kissed my neck again then rubbed his crotch against my ass. The softness of his bulge suggested the only thing he was horny for was my money. His desperation was a turn-off, but I allowed him to keep kissing my neck while I watched the unfolding depravity taking place in front of my very eyes.

Now that the scrawny dude had finished with the pig, the men who had been watching all slowly slipped away into the trees, making their way back towards the grassy field of the domain. The scrawny dude pulled his pants up and followed the others, leaving only the pig pig and baldie.

"Are you gonna fuck me again?" the pig asked him. "Cause if not then untie me so I can go home."

Baldie responded by pulling something out of his pocket and forcing it in the pig's gob before strapping something behind the pig's head. It took me a moment to realise what it was—*a ball gag!*

The pig howled a blue streak of curses around the ball in his mouth, something that sounded like, "gottamfukeengockucker!"

Baldie sniggered and slapped the pig's masked face, hard. "Thanks for the fuck, pig slut." Baldie then walked off in the direction his friends had left.

"They aren't just leaving him like that, are they?" I asked Damian who was still pashing my neck and grinding into my ass.

"Probably," came his kiss-mumbled reply.

"Why would they do that?"

"Because they've all probably fucked him so they're no longer horny."

My asshole clenched. *All of them?*

"Should we go untie him?"

"He's fine," Damian breathed out through another drunken kiss to my neck. "The dude who owns the fuck-bench will be back at some point tonight and will untie him then."

"How long will that be?"

After three more sticky little kisses to my nape, Damian rested his head on my shoulder. "Could be ten minutes. Could be five hours. The pigs know there is always a risk of being left there a while. Once you're strapped down you have no say in how long you're there for. Or what goes up your ass." His bristled chin scraped my neck as he gave my earlobe a gentle nip. "That's why I told you to be careful about coming here. You don't want one of them men strapping you to that bench. Cause they probably would if they saw a pretty young boy like you watching. Even if you tell them no."

I wasn't sure whether I believed that rapey accusation but Damian said it so casually that it sounded believable. Or at least he believed it to be true.

Stepping away from Damian's slobbery lips, I walked forward into the lit clearing. I half-expected Damian to yell out for me to come back but instead he followed me.

The pig turned his head when he heard twigs snapping beneath our feet. He moaned at us through the mask, probably trying to say *untie me*. But I ignored his moan and avoided looking him in the eyes. I stood alongside his restrained body, admiring the sight of hairy ankles and naked feet bound to the legs of the sawhorse. Sweat glinted in the dimples of his ass and the crevice of his spine, like the glint of the handcuffs around his ankles and wrists.

"He's better looking than most of the pigs who come here," Damian said as if we were observing an object. "Probably explains why there were so many up here earlier tonight."

"There were more men than what were here before?"

"Yeah, bro. This little piggy sucked more than twenty cocks tonight. And got fucked by at least a dozen of them."

I glanced at the ground and counted five cum-filled rubbers scattered around the sawhorse. If Damian was right about a dozen men making use of the pig's asshole then that still meant more than half the men had fucked him raw. And that was assuming all the rubbers were from tonight.

Damian knelt down on one knee to look the pig right in the face. "You're probably cracked out up to the eyeballs, am I right?

Got high and horny and thought you'd come here for a good time. You dumb cunt."

The pig jolted and the contorted muscles of his arms and legs drew slightly more taught, straining at the handcuffs. His bowed head snapped up right for an instant, giving me a glimpse of the ragged shock of scraggly brown hair that curled onto his neck.

"You'll regret this decision tomorrow, piggy." Damian turned his grinning face toward me and said, "That's why I don't come here if I'm too wasted. I don't want to make any dumb decisions I might regret."

I wondered what Damian considered *too wasted* because he seemed pretty wasted right now.

Damian reached over to a pile of clothes which must have belonged to the pig. He reached inside the pocket of the pants and retrieved a wallet. His thieving fingers plucked out a twenty dollar note.

"You can't take his money, Damian. Put it back."

"I'm doing him a favour."

"How is stealing his money doing him a favour?"

"Because he made a rookie mistake. Coming up to the pig pen with cash on him. Next time he will know better." Damian rubbed the cash in the pig's face. "Won't you, piggy. Oink, oink."

Damian was fucking lucky this dude was restrained because I could see the anger rippling through the pig's entire body. If the bloke got loose he would have murder on his mind. He screamed through the gag, no doubt abuse, but it came out as muffled nonsense.

"What's your name, piggy?" Damian smirked as he pulled out the man's driver's license. "Hello mister...*Kaleb Finnigan*. Nice to meet you. I see that you're a donor. Good man. That's what we like to see. Now how old are you..." Damian studied the license again. "Thirty-three. Cool. That would make you one of the younger piggies they've had up here for a while."

"How old are they normally?" I asked.

"Nearly always over forty. They usually only get younger guys if the dude is tripping off his tits...which I'm guessing is the case with Kaleb here." Turning the man's wallet around to show me a picture of a pretty brunette and two young children, Damian said, "Looks like our piggy here is a family man. I wonder if wifey knows he's out here getting dicked by old men."

I glanced down, and saw he wasn't wearing a ring, but there was a slight indentation on his finger where one would go.

Kaleb screamed again through his gag, his nostrils flaring. This was a man enraged. Truly enraged. His eyes, an icy shade of blue, were filled with aggression and the threat of violence.

Rather than back off, Damian seemed to relish in antagonising the helpless victim. He removed the ball gag so Kaleb could speak.

"I'm gonna fucking kill you, cunt," Kaleb hissed. "You thieving fucking low lives. When I get my hands on the two of you I'm gonna—"

Damian hoiked a ball of snot-tinted saliva right into the dude's open mouth.

Kaleb looked stunned, like he thought he'd been hit with a bullet. Before he could react—be it via spitting back or cursing—Damian promptly plugged his mouth back up with the ball gag.

Kaleb's arms yanked at the restraints, his head shaking about like a dying fly but eventually his Adam's apple bobbed up and down, swallowing down Damian's snot.

"I hope that was nice and tasty for ya, piggie." Damian laughed and patted Kaleb's masked face. "I have plenty more if ya hungry."

Just like I had been the night I'd paid Damian for sex, my former babysitter was on a dark power trip. Clearly even Hickford Homos had their own hierarchy, and as a bog-cruising hustler Damian must have been looked down upon by many of the men who frequented this park. But here, up in the pig pen, he was miles above any man foolish enough to assume the role of being the pig.

Standing up, Damian then walked to the other end of the sawhorse and pulled the man's ass cheeks apart so that the most secret part of his body was completely exposed and vulnerable.

I gasped at the state of Kaleb's asshole.

The hole itself was puffy and swollen, like a bee sting, turned inside-out and protruding in a slick pink nub, drenched with semen.

"That's what regret looks like," Damian said with a snigger as he dragged a finger over the gaping chasm. "If this bitch had a real pussy then he'd be knocked up."

I nodded in agreement because he expected it.

"Your ass is a little tender, isn't it, piggy?" Damian grinned as he tapped the surface of the messy hole. "That's what you get for being a dumb cunt. Stupid pig."

Kaleb moaned in shame, and as I watched, fascinated and appalled, the hole began to twitch. As if Damian had touched it with a live wire, dilating and snapping shut in a strange spastic rhythm.

"See how hairy his crack is," Damian said matter-of-factly, swiping his finger through the man's ass hairs. "That's usually a sign of a newbie. Most experienced pigs that come here shave their pussies. My guess is that Mr Finnigan ain't been the star of a show like this before and he bit off more than his pussy can chew."

Kaleb's ass suddenly burped out a murky bubble of jizz as if agreeing.

"You're lucky, piggie," Damian said, using a finger to push the discharge back inside the man's bloated hole. "He ahua mamae to nono engari ka pai."

My te reo was not great but I got the gist of it: *your sore anus will be fine.*

"Ka pai?" I blurted, pointing at the wrecked asshole, "How is that considered fine?"

"I've seen assholes in way worse shape than this. This little piggy was lucky." Damian gave the gooey hole one last tap before releasing his grip on Kaleb's ass. "At least he won't have half his ass fall out when he takes a shit tomorrow. There's been nights here when those old geezers send pigs home with a rosebud."

I stared at Kaleb's ass in sympathy. As far as male asses went it was a pretty regular man ass; a little meaty, a little hairy, a little spotty. Certainly not the sort of blemish-free bubble butt found in porn. But that's probably what made it sexy. This was the ass of a blokey bloke, a regular man. But tonight had left his hole anything but regular. It looked exactly like what the men had called it: a fuck hole. Just a place to stick your dick and drop a load.

Such a waste, I thought.

Damian reached for the front of his pants and I thought my former babysitter was about to shock me by rooting the busted hole. He shocked me instead by declaring, "I'm busting for a piss."

He held the elastic of his pants down under his balls with a casual thumb. His cock hung loose, languid and limp. He peeled back the foreskin and looked down at Kaleb's naked body. "I hope you're ready for a shower, piggy."

A stream started, a yellow arc, firm and steady. Piss splattered all over the naked man's back before Damian aimed the flow right over Damian's cummy entrance. Rivers of piss rolled down the back of his thighs, wetting the curls of leg hair.

Kaleb struggled against his restraints again, objecting to being used as a toilet. Meanwhile Damian carried on pissing all over him like it was the most natural thing in the world. After drenching the man's crack and balls, he aimed the yellow stream at his legs and feet.

I was tempted to call my former babysitter out for being disgusting, but I knew that would only make me a hypocrite considering I'd done worse to him the other night by forcing him to drink my piss.

And the truth was I didn't find it disgusting. I found it sort of sexy; in that dark, depraved way that made me ashamed.

There was something about the way Damian stood there, so casually, so unashamed, it made him so much better looking than I otherwise found him. It was masculine, raw and unapologetically male.

Damian turned around to face me as he tucked his dick back inside his pants. "What?" he said when he saw the dumbstruck look on my face. "It was just a piss. That's what he's there for."

Rather than give him the shameful compliment that the sight of him pissing aroused me, I just shook my head.

"I've been thinking," he said. "And I reckon you're hot enough not to charge. I do that sometimes. Have sex with dudes for free."

I watched his eyes fall down to my crotch when he spoke. My mouth hung open. Before I could even speak his hands were tugging me in. With a tilt of his head, he dove in at my neck. I stared dumbfounded over his shoulder while he fastened his lips on the skin of my neck. I felt his tongue. I felt the pressure of him sucking at my flesh.

I felt everything.

Our bodies were together. He made sure of that. His stomach rubbed mine through the heat of our clothes. Our legs met. A single giant hand slid around and cupped the cheek of my denim-clad ass. His strong fingers dug in. I felt the rush of his breath when he did.

Our cocks pressed against one another.

"Nngh, ah, Damian!" I blurted.

He drew his face back and I nudged at his chest with my palms. It was like trying to shove away a horse.

"I'm really flattered but..." I struggled to sputter the words. "Not here."

Damian grinned again. His eyes were on my lips when I spoke.

"Relax, man," he hummed to me. "It's just us here now. It's perfectly safe for us to kiss."

"I don't want to kiss you."

"That's not what you said the other night."

"That was different."

"Aw, go on. Just a little kiss. On the mouth."

I went to push him back, but Damian caught my wrists with a strength that I think surprised us both. He forced his body against mine, from lips to groin.

A little reluctantly—but with increasing excitement—I began to kiss him back. I figured there was no harm in us kissing. Also, I was incredibly flattered that this *mostly straight* dude was willing to get hot and heavy with me for free.

My former babysitter's lips found their way back to my neck and he slowly turned me around so that his crotch was pressing into my ass. I could feel his arousal. It had come on fast. Hard. Demanding.

Damian's arms circled my waist as his hands began fondling my junk. I swatted his hands when he undid the button of my jeans but that did not deter him. He yanked the zipper down and reached inside my boxers, groping my cock greedily.

"You have such a sexy dick, Mike. I really enjoyed sucking it the other night."

"Maybe I'll let you suck it again sometime. But not here."

He suddenly knelt down behind me and pulled my jeans past my knees. My boxers immediately followed and the warm summer breeze blew over the flesh of my buttocks.

"I thought we were just going to kiss?" I giggle-snorted, suddenly more amused than I was bothered.

"We are just kissing."

"Then why have you pulled my pants down?"

"Because I want to kiss your bum." He started peppering the smooth cheeks of my ass. I knew this was heading in the direction of rim city, and I should have stopped him, but the earlier kiss had weakened my resolve.

As I predicted, Damian's hands soon pried my cheeks apart and I could feel his eyes scrutinizing my asshole. "Damn, son. This ass looks so tasty. Can I lick it?"

"Uh...I wouldn't recommend it. I haven't showered since I got home from work so things ain't exactly fresh and sweet back there."

"That's okay," he said, then gave my moist crack a deep lick. "Boy butt ain't supposed to be fresh or sweet." *Lick.* "It's dark."

Lick. "Musky." *Lick.* "And usually very sweaty." *Lick.* "But still tastes great."

Those five licks left me quivering and had my resistance melting like butter in a pan.

Damian once again proved he was an expert at pleasing a man when his tongue dug even deeper into my shit pit. He didn't give a fuck how unclean I was. He ate my swampy ass out like he was starving, using so much force that I kept stumbling forward until eventually I was right behind the pig slut's hunched-over body. Grabbing the man's hips for support, I pushed my ass back to meet the thrusts of Damian's talented tongue. Kaleb grunted in complaint. I felt bad for using him as a leaning post but I was too excited by the whore tongue in my ass to stop.

"You taste so fucking good, Mike. So fucking good." Damian began firing spit bombs right over my hole then rubbing them in with the tip of his tongue. It seemed an odd thing to do but it felt fucking great. So did the way he ran his calloused hands up and down my legs, each finger-walking ascent ending with him giving my balls a frisky pull before gliding back down to my calves.

While I allowed myself to be licked out by a man who was practically a homeless thug, I couldn't resist the draw of Kaleb's ass and slid a hand over to his manly buttocks. I cupped the right cheek in my palm, feeling its ripe weight. My fingers slipped into the crack, grazing the hair which grew there, touching the rim of his leaky asshole. Kaleb shuffled his hips, backing his ass up onto my hand. Even though his ass pleaded for my fingers, it still felt wrong to touch him. It was exploitation, dirty, almost like rape. Besides, only a moment ago he'd threatened to kill us.

Does this dude even know what he wants?

My thoughts and hands were dragged away from Kaleb when Damian finally got to his feet again and pulled me close so we were both standing straight, both facing Kaleb's naked body. Damian turned my head and met my lips with a kiss. Even more passionate than before. If I didn't know better then I could have sworn my former babysitter had been hiding a crush from me.

"Why are you such a fucking sexy stud?" His voice was low, not quite a whisper... more of a moan. "You're making me think I might actually be queer."

I am?

That was a compliment that made my ego throb every bit as my now hard cock. Had I turned him gay? Me? Had all the blood not been rushing between my legs then I may have questioned him about it. But I was too wound up now. Too high on thinking I was a sexy stud. Even when I felt the slick tip of his bare cock rub against my ass cheeks I didn't question it, other than a simple thought of *when did he take his cock out...*

"I wish I could put my dick inside you." He pressed the tip of his cock gently at my opening. "I've never been inside anyone as hot as you. Male or female."

I half-nodded, gazing mindlessly at the pig's fucked asshole beneath me.

"Would it be cool if I put the tip in? Just the tip." His hands gripped my shoulders, massaged them gently. "So I know that I've been inside you."

My eyes rolled back when he began to massage my shoulders harder, his fingers digging into knots that were desperate to be untied.

"Just the tip," he said again, more breath than voice.

"Just the tip," I echoed.

He shifted one hand to my neck where he kept rubbing but used the other to guide his dick back to my entrance. He dragged his cock up and down my crack, teasing me with its heat and firmness. He tapped the head against my tight hole, slid it down my sweat-slick channel, and tapped me again. I got so used to the kiss-like prods that I figured that's all he'd meant when he said just the tip.

But then the sudden burn of my ass being breached swept through my nerves. I shouted in surprise. "Fuck!"

"It's just the tip, Mike," he assured me. "Just the tip."

We stood there not moving, locked in place and time, one inch of his cock inside me.

Damian started kissing my neck again and telling me how sexy I was. I lapped it up, of course. I felt him reaching around inside his pockets and seconds later he held a condom in front of me.

"Put this on," he ordered.

I wrapped up my cock, assuming we were about to trade places. Then he reached around and slathered my dick with spit, teasing me with two pumps of his hand. His free hand grasped my jaw as he spoke directly into my ear again, deep voice reverberating. "Give that slut that pretty dick of yours, Mike, and make sure the bitch feels every fucking inch."

"You want me to fuck him? The pig?"

"Mmhmm."

I stared down at the abused asshole before me, unsure if I really wanted my dick going in there, but too horny to say otherwise.

Slowly, Damian rubbed my knob up and down the length of the helpless man's hairy crack. Kaleb released a needy moan when Damian lined my cock up right over the man's gooey hole. Then, without warning, Damian thrust his hips and sank deeper inside my ass which in turn forced my cock inside Kaleb's fuck-hole.

I groaned.

Damian sighed.

The pig grunted.

Kaleb's body went rigid, but his hole was alive—squirming, squeezing, swallowing my dick in a series of spastic convulsions. It was a loose and juicy descent, and suddenly it didn't seem to matter to me that a small army of men had already conquered this married man's opening tonight. Kaleb Finnigan's cum-slick rectum still felt delicious around my cock. I released a needy whine, grateful to finally know what it felt like to be inside another man's ass.

Damian chuckled in my ear, bit it, and sank his cock deeper inside my ass.

So much for just the tip, I thought.

Damian must have had half his shaft inside me. I would have complained but I was torn by sensation at both ends; the squishy heat from some stranger called Kaleb and the burn of Damian's cock burrowing deeper inside my own ass.

My mind supplied images of him drilling into me, using me as I used the pig. For years I had fantasised about fucking a man in the ass but I never imagined it would end up happening like this. I was so overcome by the moment, and the confusion of being stuck in the middle, that I wasn't sure what to do.

Do I thrust? Grind? Bump?

The dilemma was taken out of my hands when Damian clamped a hand around my neck, pushing me forward, forcing me to drape my body over Kaleb's hunched-over form. I braced myself against the man's wet flesh; a mixture of sweat, spunk and Damian's piss.

Damian eased the rest of his dick into my chute one deliberate inch at a time while I lay stunned and balls-deep inside the pig. I may not have been a virgin back there anymore but my hole was still inexperienced enough to feel the burn. The advance of his cock seared my sphincter as it was stretched wider and wider. I bit Kaleb's shoulder to hold back the cries of pain. I knew pleasure would soon follow.

Damian finally stopped moving: he was all the way inside me, his silky pubic hair tickling the crack of my ass. The pain of his entry had waned, overtaken by the pleasurable tension of his cock buried in me.

We started moving: first Damian, thrusting his hips in steady strokes; and then me, fucking myself back on Damian before shoving my hips forward to impale Kaleb on my dick. We were quiet at first, the only sound that of his pants-clad thighs hitting my ass and the squish of my cock sliding in and out of the Kaleb's syrupy heat.

Maybe it was the position, getting fucked while I too was fucking, but it struck me that my former babysitter lacked the skill and technique of Jockey. His thrusts lacked precision, the girth of his cock not so mighty. Sure, I knew I had a cock up me but it didn't dominate the way Jockey's had.

As if reading my mind, Damian began to pick up the pace, so, too, did our noise level increase: hard breathing, grunts, gasps, and groans. Anyone walking nearby could've heard us, but at that moment I didn't care.

I mapped Kaleb's back and shoulders with my hands while I thrust, in and out, learning the planes of his muscles, the light tracing of his ribs. Clasping his back to my chest, I took a fistful of his exposed mullet in my hand and bit the back of his neck while I scuttled him like a mongrel, and he wailed into the gag. The deeper and harder I fucked the deeper and harder Damian's tool pounded my ass.

I managed to steal a glance behind me. Damian looked like a warrior king come to life, nothing but fierce determination resided on his face.

The sting of his palm clapping against my ass made me yelp. It caught me off guard.

"You like this whore dick in your ass?"

I nodded brokenly.

He chuckled, a short, barking, contemptuous sound. "I bet you do. You Pākehā fags love whores with big fat brown dicks."

His dick wasn't that big or fat but the dirty talk was working for me. Something about having a whore's cock in my ass felt transgressive, more naughty somehow. It also turned me on knowing that our history had once been so innocent, but now here we were connected by dick in ass.

He was ramming faster now, his breath chopping the air like a knife. My hands tightened into fists. I tried to ignore the burn, the ache...the pain of the taking. Instead I focused on the way my dick swam in other men's semen inside Kaleb's ass. Every thrust of my cock seemed to shake an orgasm loose bit by bit, edging me closer and closer to the completion of a moral crime.

Another slap on my ass, the other cheek this time. I cried out into the night again.

One of Damian's hands gripped my waist, the other pulled on the collar of my shirt, ripping the fabric. He collapsed on top of me, still fucking, his breath raging loud in my ear.

My sandwiched body grew tense. A small tickly feeling zapped my taint. I knew what was about to come.

"Oh... oh god, keep... o-oh..."

I didn't know if he heard me, but Damian didn't stop rooting. The tip of my cock started to spasm, and my entire lower body seized, as I flooded the condom buried inside Kaleb's mushy ass pit.

"Fuck," Daman grunted. And then he yelled it: "Fuck!" And that was the last thing he said before the animal rut took him. He fucked my ass like he probably fucked a pussy: fast and rough, with the long, swift strokes of someone sawing wood. His balls slapped against my thighs with each thrust, and his breath came fast above me, washing over me like a hot desert breeze. He pushed grunts out of me, and his own breath took on the howling tones of an animal call.

"Oh, yessss," he hissed right in my ear. He continued to press into me, his cock climbing deeper through my ass. The hardness of his flesh mashing me against the pig's piss-soaked back. I lay there, wedged between two men, one with his cock buried balls-deep inside me as it pulsated and....

Oh no. Oh no. Oh no.

The warmth started to grow. The shock froze me when I realised what was happening. Warm trickles of liquid lapped at my insides, and each time it did my asshole grew fuller, warmer....

Damian Takarangi was ejaculating inside of me!

It shouldn't have surprised me but I honestly hadn't expected it. I'd been so wrapped up with his flattery and the physical sensations at both ends of my body that I hadn't given much thought to where Damian might shoot his load. He could have pulled out and shot his load on the dirt. He could have shot it across my ass or my back. Hell, he could of rushed around and fed it to the pig.

But he chose none of those options.

The sneaky bastard was emptying himself inside of me, his cock pulsing against my asslips as it pumped out its load. Every spurt of his cock made me feel like a slut. I felt even more like a slut when his cock started to shrink inside my asshole, signalling he'd finished breeding me like a bitch.

I shuddered when he stepped back. His cock slid from my asshole, leaving me draped over the pig like a fresh kill. I felt wet and stretched and empty, hollowed out and filled at the same time.

Damian cleaned himself off using the back of my shirt and I heard him pull up his pants. I would have complained about being used as a cum rag but I was too lost in my post-orgasm haze. After a moment, I eased myself out of Kaleb's asshole and just stood there staring at the winking orifice. I could not believe I had just had my dick inside there. A total stranger. It was only when Damian clapped me on the shoulder that I finally turned around to face him.

A slow and slimy smile spread across his lips, the smile of someone who knows something wicked. "Welcome to the club, Mike. You are now officially a Hickford Homo just like me and the pig." He showed me one long, brown finger—the middle one—and walked away into the night laughing to himself.

Stood there with my pants around my ankles, I finally realised that his whole '*you could turn me queer*' spiel had all been an act. Just a way for him to prove a point. A sickly sense of Déjà vu settled over me—my vanity and thirsty ego had allowed me to be tricked once again.

Sighing in disgust—mostly with myself—I pulled the condom off and dropped it to the ground with the rest. I contemplated untying Kaleb but ultimately decided against it. That was one motherfucking angry pig under that mask and I preferred not facing his wrath. But I think the main reason I didn't want to untie him was because I didn't want to see his face. I didn't want to have it stained in my memory.

I hitched my jeans up and was about to bolt my sorry ass outta there when I heard someone say, "Was it worth it?"

I turned to look back at Kaleb, but of course his mouth was gagged. I wondered if I was imagining things. But then I heard the voice again. "You really are a slut, you know that?"

That's when I saw him. Standing in the shadows beside a kauri tree. Jockey was dressed head to toe in camouflage gear, looking like he was taking part in a military exercise.

"H-How long have you been there?" I stammered.

"Long enough for you to have some explaining to do." He had the stern look of a disappointed father. "Now come with me, slut."

Chapter 19

JOCKEY DIDN'T SAY A word to me as we walked through the domain to his parked vehicle. In fact, he didn't say a single word to me the whole drive back to his place. Each time I tried to ask him how he had known where to find me he just shook his head, giving me the silent treatment. Even after we had parked up, and walked inside his sleepout, he still didn't say anything to begin with.

Jockey fetched himself a beer from the mini fridge then went and sat down on the couch, eyeballing me as I stood awkwardly in the centre of the room. The air thickened in my imagination. Gravity doubled in weight. It was hard to focus on his face that pinned me with a hard, interrogative stare. I tried to take comfort in the fact that I was standing and he was sitting down, hoping my altitude would give me some sort of authority in the interaction that was to follow.

That hope crumbled like cigarette ash the moment he snapped his fingers and pointed to the floor, and I sat cowardly by his feet.

He took a long pull of the beer, rattled a long belch out of his stomach, and ran fingers through his sweaty hair. It was getting long—for Jockey—and it glistened under the light of the room's lightbulb.

I felt like a school child sat on the classroom floor in front of a teacher for story time. But I wasn't about to be told a story. I was about to receive a lecture. It was written all over his face. The most annoying part was I knew I deserved one.

However, I was taken back when Jockey's stern frown suddenly disappeared and he started laughing. "Of all the men in this town you could have let fuck your pussy you chose Damian fucking Takarangi. Are you insane? You just let a homeless man nut inside you."

"Damien isn't homeless."

"Maybe not this week but most weeks he is." Jockey slurped back a mouthful of beer then started looking at me icily again. "And it doesn't change the fact you let him cum inside you. And don't even think about denying it. I saw him pull out of you. He wasn't wearing a rubber, which means right now you're probably dripping his cum all through your undies inside my sleepout. Dirty bitch."

"You're the one who invited me here," I snapped back.

"I was very clear with you the other day, Mike, that I had no issue with you rooting around until the official start date of our contract. You are technically free to do what you like until Friday. *But*...I did say I would appreciate it if you play safe. I don't want to own a faggot with diseases."

His comment made me feel dirty, unclean, and very fucking angry. "You don't seem to have a problem fucking me without a condom. What's the difference?"

"Because I'm not selling my ass in Hickford Park to any Tom, Dick and Harry for drug money."

My suspicion piqued. "How do you know Damian does that?"

"Because I know things."

I couldn't decide what bugged me more; the fact he did know or how fucking smug he sounded when he said it. "But how do you know these things?"

He sighed as if I had just asked him for a kidney. "Because I'm mates with Stryder. You know...the guy you paid to bail on the threeway with Gavin?"

Jockey and Stryder being pals didn't sound right. Not based on how Stryder had acted like he barely knew who Jockey was. But that wasn't the part of what Jockey had just said that concerned me. "Stryder told you about that?"

"It doesn't matter who told me. But Stryder has talked in the past about what goes down at the park. He's pretty open about it. Including how he almost got a hiding there once from one of the other hustlers there. And it didn't take a rocket scientist to know who he was talking about when he described the guy as a crazy Māori dude who always wears the same leather jacket."

It didn't surprise me to hear this: Damian attacking the younger, prettier competition.

"Anyway," Jockey continued, "my point is I don't appreciate you skanking your pussy at Hickford Park."

"I'm not skanking my—" I took a breath to calm down. "I'm not skanking around. Okay? What you saw tonight is the only sex I've had." I then very quietly added, "Pretty much."

"What do you mean...*pretty much*?"

Jockey's piercing gaze acted like truth serum and I began to spill everything about my ill-fated night with Damian: telling him everything from how I'd got off on calling Damian a whore right down to the moment he'd assaulted me with the dildo and tied me to the bed.

"That explains your face," he said when I'd finished telling him the story. "Which I was about to ask you about."

"Yeah." I gently rubbed my sore eye. "It's getting better though."

"And even after he beat you and stole your money, you still let the prick fuck you?" Jockey laughed. "I know you're a faggot so you're short on self-respect but at least have some common sense."

"I just got caught up in the moment. I'm sorry for ruining the contract. That wasn't my intention. And I mean that."

He raised an eyebrow. "What are you on about? The contract isn't ruined. Your signature is on that piece of paper if you like it or not. And I expect you to honour it, unless you come up with the cash to buy your way out of it."

"But I thought—"

"Look, I'm not happy that you went out skanking your pussy but you aren't under my ownership until Friday. You are free to do what you like until then, no matter how much I may disapprove. While there will certainly be repercussions for what you've done, ruining the contract is not one of them. There is no way on this earth I'd let Damian dicking you take away something I have wanted for so long." His eyes settled on my crotch then back to my face. "I own you, Mike. Your ass, your cock, them sexy feet of yours... they're all mine. No one will ever know your body as well as I will get to know it. No one will ever fuck you as much as I'm gonna end up fucking you these next twelve months. You spin my wheels big time, bro. Ain't no homeless hooker robbing me of what's mine."

A normal person would have been running for the door if they heard their friend go into detail about how they viewed them as a possession—a piece of property they could fuck. But not me apparently. Sure, it worried me, more than a little, but the main thing I felt right now was wanted. Jockey Savage really wanted me, despite my indiscretions.

Jockey sniggered quietly. "I have jerked off so much this week thinking about all the shit we're gonna do together that I'm on the verge of declaring myself wankrupt."

"Wankrupt." I laughed. "That's a good one."

A long moment of silence followed. It wasn't awkward this time. Just a peaceful quiet. I wondered if the hurricane of ill-feeling had passed, or were we just in the eye of it.

Jockey broke the silence first. "I found you with the ap."

"What?"

"You wanted to know how I knew where to find you tonight. It's because I put a tracking ap on your phone when you took a shower here the other day."

"You put a tracking ap on my phone without asking me? Why would you do that?"

"Because I like to keep track of my property." he said, his eyes narrowing into slits. "Which is why I know this is the second time you've been to the park this week, so I wanted to go see why. Like, I had a suspicion you were going there for sex, why else does anyone step foot in that park at night, but I never imagined it would be with Damian."

"I said I'm sorry."

"You should be saying sorry to yourself. Damian wasn't wrong when he said you're now a Hickford Homo. And we both know you can't get much lower than that in this town."

"I know."

"You're just lucky the thought of you being a Hickford Homo turns me on," he said, adjusting his bulge. "Don't get me wrong, I will absolutely mock the fuck out of you for it until the day you die but it makes my dick hard knowing that's what you are now."

"Really?"

He nodded. "There's a reason the contract said you had to choose between becoming a Hickford Homo or getting a tattoo."

"So does that mean I've fulfilled my obligation?"

"Don't get ahead of yourself, bitch. If you recall the contract stated that I would video you being fucked and it would go online."

"Oh..."

"And after what I saw tonight I've decided if you want that option then I want to see you tied up like that poor fucker you bummed."

My leaky asshole clenched at the thought. "I don't want to do that."

"Then I guess you'll end up choosing to get the tattoo?"

I shrugged, unable to commit to either. This was the part of the contract I had struggled the most with—the way Jockey wanted to permanently taint me in some way. But it would be a lie if I didn't acknowledge how much his sadistic streak turned me on. Mostly though I envied it. I carried similar dark fantasies but unlike Jockey I just didn't have the ability to make them come true.

"So will you be getting Damian to fuck you again before Friday?" he asked.

"That is highly, highly unlikely," I replied. "If I had my way we would just start the contract early. Stop me from doing any more stupid shit and save you from going wankrupt."

"It sounds like a certain slut is still a little horny after getting fucked by a homeless man in the bushes." He finished the insult up with another swig of his beer.

Rather than snap back, like I wanted to, I resorted to flattery. "How can I not be horny when a sexy man in uniform is sat right in front of me." I reached out and rubbed his knee. "Especially when he's an alpha male with the biggest dick I've ever sucked."

"Judging by what I saw Damian pull out of your ass that's not the compliment you think it is." He flicked my hand away from his leg. "If your horny then I suggest you go back to Hickford Park. I'm not doing anything with you while you've got another man's come in your pussy."

Talk about being put in my place. Jockey's comment left me feeling dirty and small. It also made me all too aware of the soggy patch in the ass-end of my briefs.

"Speaking of which," he said. "I'd appreciate it if you take Damian to get tested at the sexual health clinic tomorrow. I want to know that he's clean."

"You can't be serious?"

"Do I look like I'm joking?" He didn't. "I told you there would be repercussions and that is one of them. Section three of the contract states I have the right to either advance or push back the start date. And so I will be pushing back the start date of our contract until I get Damian's test results."

"Why do you need Damian's?"

"Because I can't be fucked waiting thirty days so you can go get tested."

I didn't question the timeframe because the ease at which he spoke suggested he had some idea of what he was talking about. But I did question the absurdity of approaching Damian to get tested.

"And what exactly am I supposed to say to him?" I sounded like I was pleading, and in a way I suppose I was. "I can't just rock up to where he's staying and go 'hey, Damian, I'm worried you have diseases so can you go get tested.'"

"Yes you can. You can also invite him here with you afterwards. I'd quite like to watch him fuck your pussy again."

"What the fuck? You just told me that's why you won't sleep with me."

"The damage is done now. Someone may as well use your pussy until I feel it is safe to."

"Fine," I grumbled. "I'll ask him about the test. But I'm not bringing him here to have sex. I'm not lying when I said tonight was a mistake."

"That's up to you. But once the contract begins he will be invited here if you like it or not, and he will fuck you again."

"Why?"

"Because it's your duty as a faggot to respect any man who gives you the privilege of their cock. And that's very much what Damian did for you tonight. He fed that slut hole of yours the meat it so desperately needed, and for that you must always be thankful."

"But that's—"

"You have been doing your homework and looking up those websites I gave you, right? If you had then you'd know that Damian is higher up the hierarchy of men than you are."

I almost smiled when I felt a know-it-all moment coming on. "I have looked at the website. Which is why I know Damian is also a faggot, and therefore I don't have to service him."

Jockey pulled his head back and blinked. "Why is Damian a faggot?"

"Because he's been fucked before. And way more than me."

"Under normal circumstances I would agree with you, but Damian does it for cash. There is a difference. He's more like a beta bitch whose fell on tough times."

"I still don't see how that makes him higher up than me."

"How about the fact you signed a contract to let another man own your ass. Hmm? Damian hasn't done that. Damian would never do that. Only true faggots like yourself would stoop so low."

"Why are you being such a dick?"

"It's called being honest, Mike. I thought you liked that about me? Or do you only like it when the truth suits you?"

I could not decide if he had a point or was just trying to hurt me because he was jealous. Both?

"I have a responsibility as an alpha male to make you, my faggot, a better person." He sat back like he thought he was a guru. "I have skills and knowledge that you as a faggot will struggle to ever acquire, but if you're a good boy and do as your told then you might learn a thing or two."

Jockey may have been fitter than me, have a bigger cock than me, some might say he had a better sense of humour than me, but he was not smarter than me. The fact he thought otherwise was infuriating.

"And what exactly am I supposed to learn from letting Damian fuck me again?" I asked.

"You are going to learn about consequences. You will learn about regret. And you are going to learn to never disobey me again. It is the only way you will come to accept your place amongst men. It's also how you will find your freedom beneath the shame."

The words he used, and the tone he said them in, made me quickly reevaluate Jockey's intelligence.

"I can help you get to that point, Mike. And along the way I will make sure you get justice against those who have wronged you. Including Damian."

"What do you mean?"

"You're mine. And I look after what is mine." Jockey leaned forward and softly stroked the bruise on my face. "Anyone who hurts you, in any way, will eventually have to answer to me. That is what your signature on that contract guarantees you. My protection. My loyalty. My always."

More than ever before I understood the seriousness of our arrangement. Of its risks and of its rewards. We were playing a dangerous game here, like a pair of twelve-year-olds messing about with a Ouija board and summoning a dark spirit. If done right we could get answers to things we wish to know, but if we weren't careful then we risked letting that darkness ruin our lives.

About the Author

ZANE LIVES IN NEW ZEALAND in a rundown pink shack near the beach with his gaming-obsessed flatmate and a demanding cat. He is a fan of ghost stories, road trips, and nights out that usually lead to his head hanging in a bucket the next morning.

He enjoys creating characters who have flaws, crazy thoughts and a tendency to make bad decisions. His stories are steamy, unpredictable and tend to explore the darker edge of desire.

Milton Keynes UK
Ingram Content Group UK Ltd.
UKHW010948061123
432055UK00008B/358

9 798223 901822